# SUGAR PLUM SERENADE

SEAWOLF BEACH
BOOK 2

LINDA WINSTEAD JONES

Copyright © 2024 by Linda Winstead Jones

All rights reserved.

No part of this book may be reproduced in any form or by any electronic or mechanical means, including information storage and retrieval systems, without written permission from the author, except for the use of brief quotations in a book review.

Cover design by Elizabeth Wallace
http://designwithin.carbonmade.com/

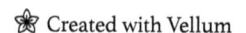

Created with Vellum

# CHAPTER 1

The gray-haired woman who'd been browsing for an hour held a bright green blouse up to her neck and studied her reflection in the full-length mirror outside the dressing room. "What do you think?"

Olive couldn't say what she thought. That shade of green was hideous. It turned the woman's skin a disturbing shade of yellow. "It's very Christmasy," she said in an easy, noncommittal tone of voice. "All that matters is what *you* think."

The customer turned this way and that, humming "Jingle Bells" as she tried to make up her mind. She stopped humming and asked, not for the first time, "Where's Dawn?"

*Not here* wasn't enough of an answer for this woman. "My sister is pregnant."

"I'm aware."

"She's due Christmas Eve, but the doctor has put her on bed rest."

The plan had been to close the boutique a couple of days before Christmas and reopen mid-January, but Dawn had been frantic about losing almost an entire month of holiday sales. Little sister to the rescue. Dawn's Radiance had been closed for a few days while Olive made plans to travel to Seawolf Beach earlier than originally planned. For the next two weeks she'd take care of Dawn's business from ten until five Monday through Friday and ten till two on Saturday.

Retail was definitely *not* her calling. Sure, she dealt with her share of difficult clients in her event planning business, but they came at her one at a time, and rarely more than one a day. How did Dawn do it? Day after day, season after season. Her big sister never seemed to lose her temper, not even with the most difficult customer. Well, she didn't admit to it, and on the occasions Olive had been in the boutique and seen her sister at work, Dawn had been amazingly calm. Olive had bitten her tongue more than once to hold back her instinctive responses, and it was just her first day.

The difficult customer for the moment handed the green blouse to Olive. "I can't decide. Will you put this back for me?"

"I'll be happy to hold it until the end of the day."

A dropped shoulder; a sigh; a tsk. Then, "Dawn always holds pieces for me for several days, if I ask. Call her. Tell her Susan Merriweather..."

"I'll hold the blouse until closing time Wednesday," Olive interrupted. If she bothered her sister with every detail that came up, Dawn wouldn't get any rest at all.

If her pregnant sister hadn't been put on bed rest, Olive would've arrived in Seawolf Beach a couple of days before Christmas to see Dawn and her husband, Mike, and their two adorable but much too energetic daughters. By then their parents would be here, exhausted but happy from their cruise. If the baby came on time, Olive would be here to see the little boy delivered and home. Three kids! How on earth was Dawn going to handle three kids and a business? She already had her hands full. Four-year-old Ava was a redheaded ball of fire. Willow was seven, also redheaded but more subdued than her little sister. Sometimes it was the quiet ones you had to watch out for.

Taking care of the boutique for a couple of weeks was preferable to babysitting. Dawn had in-laws for that, thank goodness. Olive loved her nieces, she did, but they never stopped. They were always running, chattering, and jumping. Sometimes all at once.

The downtown Seawolf Beach boutique, Dawn's Radiance, carried a variety of goods. Some were intended for tourists, but most were suitable for residents as well as visitors. Scented creams; fancy soaps; racks of pretty blouses; casual dresses as well as a few nicer ones; overpriced but very nice jeans; inexpensive jewelry and a colorful display of hats. South Mississippi in the summertime was sunny, and hats were required.

Not so much in December, when the majority of sales were Christmas presents. Jewelry, scarves, and knickknacks had made up the majority of sales today. Olive had only been tempted to kill three people. She hadn't harmed anyone, at least not yet, but she *had* imagined braining one woman with a porcelain figurine, and she'd been tempted to trip another difficult customer as she walked by. One younger woman had been so annoying, it was a good thing Dawn didn't keep a shotgun behind the counter. No, no, she didn't really think that, she wouldn't hurt a fly, but honestly, her sanity was hanging by a thread. People! Instead of buying what they wanted and leaving, they'd loitered. They'd complained. They'd argued about the prices over which, Olive informed them, she had no control.

In a perfect world she might strangle Susan Merriweather with the green blouse. If she were a violent person, which she was not. But she could imagine. There was no harm in that.

It might help matters if Olive loved Christmas the way other people seemed to. The season always put her on edge. It had been eight years since the accident that had ended her career as a dancer. She'd been performing in *The Nutcracker*. Not with a major company, just a local group in Birmingham, but at twenty-two she'd been ambitious, driven, and unfailingly optimistic. And *good*. Dammit, she'd been good. One devastating fall, and it was all gone.

*Fall* wasn't exactly the right word. Stefan had dropped her. They'd performed that lift in the Sugar Plum pas de deux hundreds of times without so much as a wobble, but not that night. He'd dropped her; she'd landed in the worst possible way. Months of physical therapy had helped immensely, but hadn't entirely restored the damage to her hip. She could walk, there was no need for a cane or painkillers, but she'd never dance professionally again.

It hadn't helped matters at all that she and Stefan had been engaged at the time. After he'd dropped her, she couldn't make herself trust him. Deep inside, she simply couldn't allow trust. She'd tried, she really had. Even if she'd managed to forgive him, he'd looked at her differently after that night. If she couldn't dance she was no longer the woman he'd fallen in love with. Whatever love they'd once shared had faded away.

Every time she heard music from *The Nutcracker*, which was everywhere this time of year, it was all she could do to keep from bolting.

These days she planned events in Birmingham and the surrounding areas. Weddings, reunions, company events, and lavish birthday parties. No Christmas parties. Not for her. Her business partner, Jessica, loved Christmas and was always happy to take on any holiday events. Olive worked very hard eleven months out of the year, but she took December off. Did she wallow? On occasion. She also visited her sister, their parents, or just rented a place at the beach or in the mountains. This year, she was on sister duty.

She could've stayed with Dawn and her family for the duration, but that house was already much too crowded. Dawn, Mike, the kids, in-laws who were there more often than not, two dogs... No. Just *no*. Olive had opted to rent a little house within walking distance of the boutique. She could even walk down to the beach on a pretty day, if she had the time. So far she had not, but then she'd spent the weekend settling into the new place.

She'd rented the two-bedroom, one-bath, blue house from Coltrane Hart, who owned a record shop and several rental houses in Seawolf Beach. He was an odd guy, but seemed nice enough. He talked to himself. Dawn had mentioned it, and Olive had seen for herself, for a short period of time. Everyone did that to some degree. She muttered to herself now and then, but with Colt it was different. Her time with Hart had been limited, she couldn't say she knew him well at all, but he'd definitely been engaged in these conversations with himself.

His girlfriend was very sweet and perfectly normal. Anna didn't seem at all concerned about Colt's odd habit of talking to air. Anna had handled all the rental details, which suited Olive just fine.

Two weeks and she'd be done here. Just two weeks. Dawn would have a new baby or else she'd be about to pop. Both sets of grandparents would be around to help, and after a couple of days to pack up her belongings and celebrate Christmas, Olive could get back to Birmingham. Everything was in motion for a New Year's Eve party in Chelsea, just south of Birmingham and not far from her condo. She'd made sure everything was in place before she left. There were a few more events on her calendar for early next year, but Jessica could handle any issues that came up.

Issues almost always came up.

With the boutique closed and locked up for the night, Olive walked. It was just a few blocks to her rental house on Jasmine Street, and she was bundled up in a new jacket she'd purchased at Dawn's Radiance. Dawn had told her to take what she wanted, since she'd refused a salary for her time in Seawolf Beach, but she'd paid. Full price. Soon she was on the tree-lined street walking to the blue house, which stood out against the larger white and yellow homes. Her rental was the smallest on the block, but it wasn't an eyesore by any means. It was quaint. Charming. And temporary.

Two weeks.

Olive stood on the small porch, keys in hand, ready for a night in. Maybe a movie on TV and one of the frozen dinners she'd purchased when she'd stocked up for her stay. She wanted peace and quiet, her feet up, maybe some cookies after that frozen dinner...

She jumped when a man's voice interrupted her introspection.

"Welcome to the neighborhood, Olive Carson."

Those were not alarming words, the tone of voice was easy and friendly, and he knew her name. Was that good or bad? She turned to face the man who stood in the yard.

*Him.*

"Thanks," she said. "I'm just here for a few weeks."

"Mike told me. Nice of you to help while Dawn is out of commission."

She'd met Nate Tucker three times in the past few years, during quick trips to Seawolf Beach to see her sister. Christmas; a summer barbecue; during a fall music festival. He was one of those laid-back, easygoing guys with a charming smile and no apparent ambition. Nice body, a bit of stubble on a strong jaw, dark blond hair, blue eyes. She'd noticed those eyes before, in their brief interactions at Dawn's house. They were lively, striking, mischievous. Women stared as he walked by, and with good reason. You might even say some swooned. She did not swoon. Ever. This guy looked like trouble walking.

"They're family," she said. "I'm happy to help." Which was only kind of a lie. She loved her sister, but why was she having a baby at Christmas? Olive was usually able to ignore most of the holiday season, and enduring a couple days of forced holiday cheer with family was bearable. It didn't last long. This year, however...

Tuck — everyone called him by a shortened version of his last name — jerked a thumb at the big white house next door. She'd walked past it on her way in and had admired the structure, and the fact that unlike the other houses on the street he had zero Christmas decorations on the exterior of his house. She hadn't bothered with lights or wreaths, either. After all, she wouldn't be here long. Anyone driving or walking past would peg them as two Scrooges, side by side.

"If you need anything while you're here, give a shout and I'll do what I can."

She wouldn't need anything from this too good-looking, overly-friendly man. He was just being polite. Men like this one were always taken by some woman or another. Or more than one. Unless something had changed since she'd seen him last, Tuck spent his nights in the bar he owned. The Magnolia, located on the other side of the highway, looked like a dive on the outside, but there must be some appeal. Whenever she drove past it was always packed. There was live music most nights, Mike had told her the one time he'd tried to convince her to go there.

No thanks.

"Thank you. I'm sure I'll be fine." With that she turned away and inserted the key in the lock, twisted it, and opened the door. She immediately backed out onto the porch again, stumbling a little as she escaped the horror. "Oh my God, someone broke in!"

"What?" Tuck ran up the steps, passed her, and stuck his head inside. "What's wrong? Everything looks fine to me."

Olive pointed past him to the offending object. "*That* wasn't here when I left this morning."

Tuck looked down at her. She didn't remember him being this tall, but then he'd never been quite this close before. "The Christmas tree?"

She nodded.

The offending tree was maybe four feet tall, and it sat on a side table in front of a small window in the living room. If she'd walked around the house instead of straight to the front door, she would've seen the tiny white lights reflecting off small gold balls through that window.

Tuck walked inside and straight to the tree. He picked up a piece of paper, which had been placed beneath the tree like an unwanted gift. He read the note silently, soon breaking into that easy smile of his. "Mike. He said the girls wanted to surprise you. They insisted Aunt Olive needs a Christmas tree."

Aunt Olive did *not* need a Christmas tree.

If not for Willow and Ava, she'd take the tree down immediately, but it was likely they'd be in the house at some point while she was here. It would hurt their feelings if she removed this reminder of the holidays they'd gone to such pains to give her.

"Well, I am definitely surprised," Olive said as she walked inside the house. She turned and looked up at her temporary neighbor. "Thanks. I guess I'm on edge today. Retail is new to me. I mean... *people*."

He laughed. Dammit, it was a nice laugh. "I hear you. I deal with a different crowd, but the public is the public no matter where they are."

"I suppose that's true." Would it be rude to shoo him out the door? With an audible "shoo" and a wave of her hands? Probably.

"You should come by The Magnolia tonight," he said, and then he turned and walked toward the open front door. "We don't serve anything fancy, but the chef makes a mean burger, and the fries are crispy and salty. After a day of retail, a glass of wine might be just the thing. A good local band will be there tonight playing seventies and eighties covers, mostly. They start at eight, if you're interested."

She was not. She planned to be in her pajamas well before eight.

"Maybe if you stop by, I can convince you to dance with me."

There were a hundred ways she could say no, a hundred *better* ways, but she blurted out, "I don't dance."

Tuck turned in the doorway. "Never?"

"Never," she whispered.

There was that easy smile again. "That's a real shame. Maybe one of these days I can change your mind." Before she could say no again, he added, "Come by any time, neighbor."

The door closed, and Olive was left alone with a four-foot artificial tree with tiny white lights and gold ornaments. She studied it for a moment. The tree was pretty, with the lights and the sparkling gold. She hadn't had a tree of her own for years. Not since the accident.

"Think of it as an artificial houseplant," she said aloud, talking to herself as Colt Hart did. It didn't matter. No one was here to see or hear. "With a little extra light, since it gets dark so early this time of year."

Olive turned her back on the tree and slipped off her jacket as she walked toward the kitchen. She only had one other thing to say to herself.

"Bah, humbug."

∼

ON A MONDAY NIGHT The Magnolia wasn't packed to the rafters, but a nice mix of locals and tourists made for a decent crowd.

Tuck left his full-time bartender, Ginny, in charge and his old faithful cook, Terrence, in the kitchen, doing his thing and doing it well. No one could say The Magnolia had an extensive menu, and anyone looking for a healthy meal would be sorely disappointed, but the burgers, fries, and a couple of specialty sandwiches sold well.

When the band started playing, Tuck closed himself in his office and listened. The sounds were muted, but he could hear well enough as he took care of some boring but necessary paperwork. The local band was good, they entertained the customers, but they needed a new lead singer.

Not that he'd tell them so.

While he took care of work that had become almost mindless, he thought about Olive Carson. Damn, she was pretty. Sleek dark hair; chocolate brown eyes; killer body. Gorgeous or not, something was off. Who was frightened of a little Christmas tree? He supposed it was the idea that someone had been in her house that spooked her, not the actual tree, but she had skirted around the thing like it was a coiled snake.

Maybe she disliked the holidays as much as he did.

He had good memories of Christmases as a child, but after his mother's death there hadn't been another good one. His dad's younger brother, Houston, had taken care of him, that was true enough. He hadn't thrown his thirteen-year-old nephew out to fend for himself. During those years Christmas Eve had been spent here, in The Magnolia, with lonely drunks and sad music on the jukebox for company. Merry Christmas, indeed.

Dwelling on the past was a waste of time. He'd rather think about his new neighbor than maudlin memories. He'd met her a time or two before, it wasn't like she was entirely *new*, but on previous occasions they'd been in a crowd, at some kind of gathering at Mike Woodward's house. Of course he'd noticed that Mike's sister-in-law was pretty, but something about seeing her earlier today, going to her rescue even though she hadn't needed rescue from a Christmas tree, struck him in a different way. Otherwise she wouldn't be on his mind even now. He wouldn't be sitting here thinking about her, bothered that she didn't dance. Why not?

He shook off the questions. It sure as hell wasn't any of his business.

Ginny knocked on the door and then opened it without waiting for a response. "I gotta run. My kid threw up all over the sitter, and she's having a come apart. You good to cover the bar for a bit?"

"Sure." They'd be closing in a couple hours, and there were times he actually liked the bartending part of the job. Working behind the bar was rarely boring, though it did get old after a while. As Olive had said... people.

As he approached the bar the band started a new song, one that had been requested by a drunk who sat at a table near the foot of the stage. "Merry Christmas, Baby."

Tuck smiled, but under his breath he muttered, "Bah, humbug."

# CHAPTER 2

Olive opened her eyes much too early on the morning of her second day in retail. She tried to go back to sleep, but that wasn't happening. This was an unexpected and new situation for her, temporarily living in a new place and taking over the boutique for a couple of weeks. The thoughts that came with all that kept her awake. She'd never done well with change. And yet that's what life was, apparently. Constant change.

There were always things to do before she unlocked the boutique door at ten. Cleaning, organizing, a little paperwork. But no matter how much work was waiting for her, no matter how early she'd awakened in the strange bed, there was no reason to get to Dawn's Radiance two hours ahead of time.

She crawled out of bed, stumbled to the kitchen, and made a single cup of coffee. The house had come fully furnished and included a small coffee maker that took pods. Not her favorite method of preparation, but it would do. With caffeine kicking in she pulled on a pair of sweats and a long-sleeved T-shirt and headed out, locking the door behind her. It was a little brisk, but the cool air felt good. Invigorating.

As she walked past Tuck's house, she couldn't help but

glance in that direction. All was quiet, as if the house and everyone and everything in it slept. It didn't seem to be his style, not at all. She would've pictured him in an efficient apartment, or a modern house, or a small cottage. This house... it was kind of magnificent. It had been built for a family. Did he have one she didn't know about? A wife, kids, holidays and birthdays celebrated with style. But as far as she knew, Tuck was alone. Unattached.

His truck, a fairly new gray monstrosity, was parked in the driveway. He worked at night, kept hours that suited his business, so he was probably sleeping soundly. Alone?

A weird sensation swept over her, sending a chill down her spine. Not her business. She didn't care.

The other houses she passed before she turned toward the beach all sported Christmas decorations. Some were small and tasteful. A wreath. A little bit of festive garland on a banister. Others had gone all out with lights and inflatable Santas and snowmen. One of the Santas had lost some air and sagged a bit.

The walk from her turn at the end of the street to the beach was relatively short. If she was going to live near the water she might as well take advantage of it. This wasn't good weather for swimming or sunbathing, but the gulf was magnificent no matter what time of the year it was.

Olive took off her shoes and left them behind to walk toward the water, enjoying the feel of cool sand between her toes, the sound of the waves, the scent of salt water. The sun was barely up; the soft light was perfect, a gentle welcome to a new day.

She'd been overthinking the situation she found herself in. Yes, everything was different this year, but she could make this a good day even if it was getting close to Christmas. She could make all the days during her stay in Seawolf Beach good ones, if she adjusted her thinking a little. If she could just let go.

One of these days she was going to have to leave her distaste of the holiday behind. She knew it, told herself that every year. And yet on some winter days she wallowed and threw herself a pity party. Why? Wallowing wasn't good for anyone.

She had the beach and the magnificent view before her to herself, until a runner approached at a slow, steady pace. No shirt in this weather. And shorts! Movement probably kept him warm enough, but to her he *looked* cold. As he drew closer, she recognized Coltrane Hart. He looked serious, focused... and he wasn't talking to air this morning, as he so often did.

Colt smiled and slowed as he approached. When he wasn't acting weird, he was pretty appealing. Handsome, with a runner's body and a nice smile. It was hard to focus on that when he was fully dressed and talking to himself.

"How's everything with the house?" he asked as he came to a stop a few feet away.

"Great," she said. "I love it."

"Good. If you need anything, anything at all, give me a call."

"Thanks." She'd be more likely to contact his fiancée if she needed anything, but still, the offer was nice. "Anna doesn't run with you?"

"Anna isn't a morning person." Colt smiled, and his affection shone through. His love was evident in the way he said *Anna*, and in the warm gleam in his eyes.

It had been a long time, but she didn't think Stefan had ever looked this way when he said her name. So why the hell did she still think about him, *at all*?

"Dawn told me about your engagement a while back," she said. "When's the wedding?"

"Spring." He looked out at the water. "Probably right here, or close by. I'd be happy to get married today, anywhere, any time, but Anna's mom wants a real wedding for her daughter. That's not too much to ask, I guess."

He had to be getting cold, since he'd stopped running.

Besides, talking about weddings made her itchy. "I need to head back and get ready for work. Enjoy your run. Tell Anna I said hello."

"Sure thing." Colt waved again and jogged on. Olive turned away and walked through the sand, back toward her shoes and home. Home for the moment, anyway. She might have to adjust her opinions about the record store owner/landlord. This morning he'd seemed perfectly normal.

She almost laughed at herself. What was normal?

~

TUCK KNEW Colt Hart pretty well. It was a small town; they were both members of the Seawolf Beach Business Owners' Association; they had mutual friends. For a short while they'd been neighbors, after Tuck had bought the Jasmine Street house and before Colt had decided to rent out the small blue house next door. Even then, their work hours had been so different they rarely saw one another. Colt didn't get out much, so he wasn't a regular at The Magnolia. Tuck didn't own a record player, so he hadn't been inside Hart's Vinyl Depot for years. Last time he was here, he'd stopped in for coffee. That had been years ago, not long after he'd moved back to town.

The record store was busy for a Tuesday, as was much of downtown Seawolf Beach. It was nice that so many shopped locally, and that vacationers took advantage of the uniqueness of the town's shops and restaurants. Come January all business would be slow. At least, that was usually the case. March would bring a change. With a warmup in the weather, the tourists came.

As he had last time, Tuck stopped by for the coffee before an afternoon of his own Christmas shopping. A high school kid, Benny, manned the coffee bar. It wasn't yet four o'clock, so it was possible Benny had come straight to the depot after school, getting in a few extra work hours to earn money for the holidays. Since it was a cool 62 degrees outside, several people had the same idea. Coffee. Not for the first time, Tuck thanked his lucky stars that Uncle Houston hadn't left him a business anywhere north of Mississippi. He wasn't sure his thin blood could take it.

Tuck had no family, not since his uncle's death. He could live anywhere. Sell The Magnolia, pack up, get out of town. He'd thought about it more than once, but this was home. He'd tried to deny that for a few years, but Seawolf Beach was in his blood, thin as it was.

Helen Sommers manned the counter, greeting and taking care of a steady stream of customers thrilled with their finds. Music from another era played over the speakers. The song currently playing was too old for Tuck to identify, but it was nice enough if you liked that kind of thing.

Colt stood near the front counter, talking to himself. Some people made a big deal out of that, but Tuck considered it a harmless quirk. After a couple minutes of chattering to no one, Colt turned his back to the room. It was apparent he continued to speak. Might be less obvious if he wasn't currently using his hands to emphasize a point.

Tuck took his coffee and sat on one of the old depot benches. The music that filled the room was old, that was sure, but it was also oddly soothing. Music could do that. Over the years he'd found that a song could sometimes change the mood of a crowd or of a single person, for good or... not. As he sat there, sipping coffee and letting his thoughts wander, his mind turned to his new neighbor.

Olive Carson wasn't really a neighbor. She was temporary, a short-term renter. She could've stayed with her sister and family while she was here, but having met her a time or two he understood why she'd chosen to book her own place. Olive wasn't unfriendly, but she was quiet. Reserved, even. Mike and Dawn's home was always a madhouse, with those two girls and the dogs. Mike wasn't much better than a big kid himself. Every time Tuck had been in that house, there had been turmoil.

Olive was the opposite of turmoil.

It was perverse of him, he knew it, but ever since she'd said she didn't dance he'd been determined to get her on the dance floor. Just once. That's what he wanted for Christmas, one turn around The Magnolia dance floor with a beautiful woman who said she didn't dance.

Everyone danced.

Colt spun around and walked to Tuck, said hello, then sat on the opposite end of the bench. There was no smile, not today. He didn't speak right away, but he did lift his hand as if to silence someone who wasn't there.

"Humor me," Colt said, looking directly at Tuck.

"Okay." Maybe the owner of the depot was quirkier than he'd realized.

"What was your mother's name?" Colt asked.

The personal question came out of the blue. Tuck's heart hammered hard, in response. How long had it been since anyone had mentioned his mother? No one had ever asked for her name; at least, not for a very long time. "Doreen," he answered. "Doreen Tucker."

He hadn't thought about his mother for years, not in any deep and meaningful way. Sure, now and then a good memory would come to him, and in that moment he missed her. A lot. He wished she'd lived longer. They hadn't made enough memories. He'd been born late in her life, at a time when she'd thought there was no chance she could have a baby. She'd died two months after his thirteenth birthday. His father was already gone at that point, dead for five years.

After his mother's death he'd moved in with Uncle Houston,

moving from a small town in western Tennessee to Seawolf Beach, where he'd stayed for a few years before joining the Army.

Hardly a heartwarming tale.

Colt bolted off the bench, talking to himself as he walked to the back room. Okay, that was weird. You'd think a recently engaged man with a hot girlfriend would try to get rid of his bad habits. Still, if Anna didn't care about her fella talking to himself, why should he?

He didn't.

Talking about his mother stirred up memories he could do without. Christmas mornings alone. Manning his bar where other lonely people went on Christmas Day. Not that he was lonely, not really, but the truth was he envied Mike his hectic household. Even Colt, off-center as he was, had a fiancée this year.

Something tickled his right cheek. Tuck swatted at what he assumed was a bug, hoping it wasn't a spider. He hated spiders. Whatever it was, the bug moved on.

He finished his coffee, stood, and headed for the exit. Maybe he didn't have a family or a hot fiancée, maybe he'd be on his own again this year, or at someone else's home for Christmas trying not to feel like a fifth wheel. He didn't want much; he didn't need what he didn't have.

Best to keep it simple. All he wanted for Christmas this year was a dance.

~

CUSTOMERS HAD BEEN in and out of the boutique all day, and thank goodness it had been a mostly happy crowd. Olive hadn't been tempted to strangle or trip anyone. She credited her early morning walk on the beach to her own improved mood.

Maybe she could get used to this retail gig. Temporarily, of course.

Christmas spirit ran rampant through Seawolf Beach. Several of the customers knew one another and visited as they shopped. They discussed upcoming parties, cookie recipes, and school holiday programs. A concert, a play, a group of carolers. It was almost enough to make Olive look at Christmas differently. *Almost.*

Susan Merriweather returned for her green blouse, which she said she'd dreamed about the night before. Even she was pleasant. Things were looking up.

One young woman had been noticeably stressed, but when with Olive's help she found just the right gift for her mother, she relaxed, smiled, and left Dawn's Radiance with a spring in her step.

Olive's own parents would be here a few days before Christmas. They'd offered to come help with the girls when Dawn had to go on bed rest, but that would've meant cancelling their long-planned cruise and with Mike's folks and Olive here, it wasn't necessary.

She had the feeling Mike didn't consider his in-laws all that much help. Olive couldn't really argue with him on that point. Her parents were free spirits, retired travelers. They found fun wherever they went. The December cruise had been on their calendar for a while, but any time of the year they might decide on a whim to travel someplace new. With a map and no plans whatsoever, they'd hit the road.

She'd wondered more than once if she was adopted.

With less than an hour until closing time, the crowd thinned. Olive had plans for her evening. First a stop by Dawn's house to check on everyone, then she'd swing by that little restaurant she liked so much and get a big salad to go. Pajamas, a little TV, a couple chapters of her book, then blessed sleep. Tomorrow she'd start all over again. If the weather cooperated, maybe she'd get in another walk on the beach before work.

She was rearranging a rack of blouses in the back of the room when the bell over the door jingled. Drat! There were just a few minutes until closing time. She gave a mental double drat when she saw who'd walked in.

Tuck was a friend of Mike's, a good neighbor who didn't mind rushing into her house to save the day when she thought she'd been reverse burgled. But he also made her itchy all over. No, those were *not* pleasant tingles. The itchiness had to be a warning of some sort. Olive was a cautious person. She never ignored a warning.

"I can't imagine there's anything here in your style," she said as she approached the counter.

Tuck looked up, down, all around. "Very funny, Ms. Carson. As I'm sure you know, I'm not shopping for myself. I need a few Christmas presents."

Of course he did. She'd thought earlier that he was single, but a guy like this one must have a girlfriend. Maybe more than one. Did he have family to buy for? Mother, sisters, aunts. She didn't know him well enough to be sure. "Are you looking for anything in particular?"

"Something pretty."

That wasn't helpful. "Who are you buying these gifts for?"

He shrugged his shoulders. "Just... women."

*Just women* wasn't at all helpful. "You're going to have to be more specific." Today had gone well and she felt like she was getting into a groove, but in the end retail was definitely *not* her thing.

Tuck walked to the back of the store where there was a big display of scarves and hats. "Who are you shopping for?" she asked, just a little bit testy. She hoped frustration didn't show in her voice, but that was a wasted hope.

He removed one pretty blue scarf from the rack, then a springy looking flowered one. He checked out the prices. The scarves were very nice and *not* cheap, but he didn't flinch. No, he tossed the two scarves over his shoulder, then randomly grabbed six more and walked to the checkout counter.

"You want all of these?" Olive asked. She didn't get a commission, she wasn't getting paid at all, but this was Dawn's business and with two kids, soon to be three, she needed her boutique to thrive. It would be foolish to question a good sale.

"I might be back for more," he said as he dropped the scarves onto the counter. "Oh, can I have one of those fancy little Dawn's Radiance bags for each scarf?"

"How many girlfriends do you have?" Olive blurted. Whoops. Mistake. She did *not* care...

"Zero, at the moment," Tuck answered.

Hmm. She shouldn't be so curious. It was none of her business. Still, she asked, "Sisters?"

He shook his head. "Nope."

"Aunts? Cousins?"

He smiled, sending a maddeningly charming grin in her direction. "You really want to know who these scarves are for, don't you?"

"I couldn't care less," she said as she rang up the purchases.

He laughed, a little. It was a nice laugh, she had to admit. "You don't play poker at all, I suspect. Your face tells everything, Olive Carson."

It wasn't the first time she'd heard that accusation.

"I'm practicing the art of carrying on meaningful conversations with customers. I'm new at it, so... forget everything I said." Judging by the expression on his face, Tuck didn't, *wouldn't*, forget anything.

"I'm a volunteer firefighter," he said. "Every year at Christmas we collect gifts for those who might not have much or hell, anything without help. This year we're running a little low on gifts for the older ladies on the list."

"I don't want to ruin a sale, but you can probably buy a hundred scarves at Walmart for what you're paying here for eight."

Tuck leaned on the counter, moving in a little, not quite invading her space but looking as if he might. "I could, but Christmas gifts should be special. Imagine the excitement when a woman who expects nothing gets a little Dawn's Radiance bag with a beautiful, extravagant scarf inside."

Oh, no. This was awful. Tuck wasn't just hot. He was more than handsome and charming and chivalrous. He was *nice*.

"What about your family? Anyone there you need to shop for?"

"I don't have any family," Tuck said.

*Foot, meet mouth.* "Sorry. I shouldn't have…"

"No worries."

He was quiet while she wrapped each scarf in tissue paper and placed it in its own small bag. From her experience, Tuck was never quiet. He said *no worries*, but he looked a little worried to her. Family must be a sore subject.

When she finished bagging the final scarf, her last customer of the day got a text alert and pulled his phone out of his pocket. He read the text, but didn't bother to answer. "I had no idea it was so late. I've kept you past closing time."

"I don't mind sticking around for a good sale," she said. "Don't you need to answer your text?"

He shook his head and put the phone back in his pocket. "It can wait. I really do feel bad about keeping you here late. Let me buy you dinner to make up for it."

Olive almost blurted out a quick *no*, but something stopped her. She complained about her family all the time. Her mother was always telling her what to do. Advice flowed freely, and for the past five years or so, constantly. She was constantly arguing with her mom that she *wasn't* stuck, that she *didn't* need to move on.

Dawn had a pretty much perfect life, but that life was so chaotic too much time together eventually made Olive crazy. Her dad... she loved her dad but he was overly protective. And forgetful. And he told the *worst* jokes. But they were her family and she loved them, warts and all.

Tuck had no one. How was that possible? She wanted to know. Against all reason, she wanted to know more about Nate Tucker.

"Why not?" What did she have to lose?

## CHAPTER 3

It wasn't a date, Olive told herself as she stored Tuck's purchases behind the counter. He was a friend, a neighbor. That was it. She'd only be in Seawolf Beach for a couple of weeks, so it would be foolish to date anyone. So, it wasn't a date.

The weather was a little chilly, but still, the walk was pleasant. It was nice to move forward instead of walking in circles in the limited space of the boutique. Tuck asked about her day; she shared only the good. Pleasant customers. Sales. It was just her second day, but she was learning her way around. She asked about his day, but he didn't share much. Good business for a Tuesday afternoon at the bar and no fires to call out the Seawolf Beach Volunteer Fire Department had made for his own good day.

They didn't have far to walk. Tuck led her to a small, white, one-story house just beyond what was considered downtown. The only sign that it was a restaurant was the hand-painted placard on the front porch. *Maggie's*. Dawn had never mentioned this place, and Olive was certain she never would've found it on her own.

They stepped inside, and she immediately realized why

Dawn had never said anything about Maggie's. White tablecloths. Waiters in dark suits and pristine white aprons. Soft, unobtrusive music playing in the background. This was not the place to bring two little girls. There were probably no chicken nuggets or mac and cheese on the menu.

She started to tell Tuck that she was underdressed for a place like this, but a glance proved her wrong. Every customer in the restaurant was as casually dressed as she and Tuck were.

Her escort approached the wait stand. "I don't have a reservation, but I thought maybe on a Tuesday it would be safe to take a chance."

The pretty young blonde smiled at him, the way women probably did on a daily basis. "We always have a place for you, Tuck." The hostess grabbed two menus and led them to a back corner. As they walked through the restaurant, Olive glanced through a couple of doorways into other rooms. Maggie's was bigger than it appeared to be from outside.

This wasn't a place you brought a neighbor for a friendly meal, but was the perfect place for a *date.*

They were seated at a corner table that would've been great for a romantic dinner. It was almost private. A new itch crawled up her spine. A warning? Maybe.

Olive studied the menu. Maggie's wasn't cheap by any means, but it wasn't as expensive as she'd expected. As she perused her choices, she said, "I'll be paying for my own meal."

"No, no, I invited you…"

She lowered the menu just enough to glare at Tuck over the top. "You tricked me. This is *not* a date. We're just friends having dinner together. That's it."

"Are we?" he asked. "Friends?"

"I suppose." She turned her attention to the menu. So many choices! After a long day of retail, she was starving.

"Can't one friend buy the other one dinner?"

"Not tonight," she said without looking at him again.

"Fine. Be that way. If you change your mind, let me know."

She wasn't going to change her mind.

She chose shrimp and grits; Tuck ordered a steak. Fresh baked bread and salads were placed before them, and again, Olive was reminded of how hungry she was. Maybe if she attacked her food like a starving dog, Tuck would be glad this wasn't a date. He could definitely have a steady girlfriend or a wife if he wanted one, so he must be particular. Did this laid-back, easygoing guy have high standards? Would a little crude behavior in a nice restaurant make him back off?

Did she want him to back off?

Not really. Besides, she couldn't make herself misbehave in public.

Over bread and salad, he quizzed her. *What do you do when you're not helping your sister? Do you enjoy being an event planner? Is there a boyfriend at home?* He already knew where she lived, from their past brief encounters at Dawn's house. She knew it was coming, but she still twitched a little when he said, "Mike tells me you used to be a ballerina. That's cool."

"Enough about me," she responded without addressing that issue. "What do you do with yourself in Seawolf Beach?"

He narrowed one eye but didn't press her about her old vocation. "You know everything there is to know about me. I'm a simple man living a simple life. I'm thirty-four years old and have all my teeth. No cavities. I own The Magnolia, the bar Uncle Houston left to me when he passed a few years back. In case you're not aware, the place isn't as fancy as the name implies. I'm also a volunteer firefighter, but thank goodness that doesn't take a lot of time. Though we do train on a regular basis. There was a big fire a couple months back but nothing since, not even a dumpster fire. We have to stay sharp, prepared for anything."

"I had no idea about your excellent dental health," she said with a smile. "I guess I did know the rest, or most of it. And no girlfriend?"

"I already answered that question. No. Not at the moment."

She wanted to ask *why not*, but she didn't. Was there a recent heartbreak? Was he difficult in a way she hadn't yet seen? "The Magnolia must be open tonight. Why aren't you there?"

"I'd rather be here, with my *friend*."

Olive glanced down at her salad.

He continued. "I have employees who can handle the place if I need a night off, especially on a weeknight. I'm always there weekends, though, that's when the place is busiest." He looked at her in a disturbingly direct way. "We have live bands several nights a week. Music brings in the crowds. Some come to listen, others to dance the night away. You were a ballerina, so why don't you dance?"

She was saved from answering when a waiter appeared to take away her salad plate and deposit shrimp and grits before her. The bowl was massive! She'd never finish it all. Tuck's steak, baked potato, and green beans were placed before him. He didn't even look at the plate; he waited for her to answer.

Fine. Why not? "I thought maybe Mike told you that, too. I had an accident. My hip was messed up big-time, and that was that."

"Car?"

"No."

"What happened?"

She looked him in the eye. Sometimes blunt was the way to go. "I was dancing the Sugar Plum pas de deux at the annual production of *The Nutcracker*. My partner, who was also my fiancé at the time, dropped me mid-lift. I landed badly."

He winced, then shook it off. "So, who killed him for you?"

The question made her smile. "Sadly, no one."

"Does it hurt?"

"No, though on occasion I can tell you when rain's coming, like an eighty-year-old with bad knees."

"If it doesn't hurt, why don't you dance? Not ballet, maybe, I can see that, but... for fun."

He was relentless! Olive sighed and wagged her fork in his direction. "Eat before your food gets cold. That's what I'm going to do." She dug into her shrimp and grits and almost moaned in pleasure, it was so good.

Tuck ate his own meal, dropping the interrogation. Olive's mind continued to spin. His questions stirred up thoughts best left buried. Stefan. The injury. Why didn't she dance anymore? Saying it aloud did make the ban sound silly. She loved music, and it was only natural to move, to embrace music fully, to let it flow through her.

The answer was simple enough. She didn't dance because she was always afraid someone would drop her again.

Tuck walked her home, which made sense since they were neighbors. It was a pleasant night, for December. Chilly, but not cold. Their street was quiet, peaceful, so unlike her own neighborhood. Tonight she even liked the Christmas tree lights that twinkled in other neighbors' windows.

She was only a little annoyed that he'd slipped his credit card to the waiter while she'd been distracted. It was a nice gesture. She'd return the favor at some point while she was in town.

Her new friend didn't turn and wave when they reached his house; he stayed beside her, escorting her all the way home. He even walked up the steps to the front door and stood there while she fished the key out of her purse and unlocked the door. Then she turned to face him, intending to offer a simple thanks.

"If this was a date, I'd kiss you good night," he said.

Her stomach fluttered. She did not have time for butterflies! "Good thing it wasn't a date, then."

He didn't move in, but he didn't turn away, either. "Is it though? Is it a good thing?"

"Friends, right?" she whispered.

"I already have plenty of friends."

That simple statement made Olive hold her breath for a long second. He wanted more. So did she, though she was reluctant to admit it even to herself. She could lean in and up and kiss him, but she waited too long.

"Good night, Olive," he said as he turned and walked away.

The moment was gone before she even realized it was a moment.

∽

TUCK GLANCED at Olive's house as he cranked up his truck and headed out. She'd already be at the boutique. He'd stop by Dawn's Radiance this afternoon and pick up the scarves he'd bought, maybe ask her to dinner again. Before that he had work to do at The Magnolia. Running a bar was more than playing bartender when he felt like it. It was ordering, remodeling, paperwork, maintenance, organizing entertainment, managing his handful of employees, cleaning when the housekeeping crew didn't do a good job of it. There was always something.

He liked Olive; he'd thought about her all night. There might've even been a dream that had faded as he'd come fully awake. She was different from the other women he'd dated in the past few years. Even though she'd insisted last night wasn't a date, it had sure felt like one.

In the past three or four years he'd met a few women in The Magnolia and had started relationships that didn't go anywhere. He'd bet his last dollar Olive had never set foot in a bar like his.

She was quiet most of the time, almost reserved. It was unlikely she'd ask him out to dinner, or for anything else. Olive Carson wasn't one to make the first move. She was a stubborn "I can do it myself" person, through and through.

She wouldn't be here long. When Christmas was over, she'd be gone. Obsessing about her was stupid. He should know better. It was a waste of time to think about a kiss, a dance, and to be honest a whole lot more.

He hadn't yet reached the highway when his cell rang. The phone was in a holder on the dash, so it was easy to check out the caller. Hmm. The only time Colt ever called him was about business owner's association crap. A problem, an election, a code violation. This close to Christmas everyone was swamped, so he couldn't imagine why Colt would call.

There was only one way to find out. He punched the green button to answer. "What's up?"

"Are you busy?" Colt asked.

"On my way to work."

"Could you swing by before or maybe after..." There was a pause. Colt whispered in the background, but Tuck could make out a couple of words. *Patient.* And a disgusted *fine.* "Before work would be best," Colt said when he returned his attention to Tuck. "If you can make it."

"Sure. I'll be right there." He changed course and headed for the depot, which wasn't much more than a block away, parking in the back near the railroad tracks to leave the premium street parking for paying customers. The back door was sure to be locked, so he walked around the building, down the sidewalk, and through the front door.

Quite a few customers browsed, flipping through albums, excited when they found what they were looking for, disappointed when they didn't. Today it was Colt's girlfriend, Anna, who ran the coffee bar. Benny would be in school this time of day. Anna looked Tuck's way and her smile faded, then came back again a bit brighter than before. Maybe a bit *too* bright.

"Colt's in the back," she said. Which meant she knew he'd come in because his presence had been requested.

The back half of the depot was almost as large as the front, but it wasn't nearly as interesting or as organized. The lights were dimmer; the floor and the walls were plainer; the doorways to offices or storage rooms were mostly closed. To be honest, it was kind of a mess back here. Tuck liked his own storerooms tidier than this. Even though he'd discovered early on that he wasn't suited to the military, his time in the Army had drummed a sense of order into him, he supposed. That desire for order helped him run his business in ways he'd never expected.

Colt waited by an old depot bench that was in need of repair and a good sanding and coat of varnish. Three cases of bottled water had been stored on that bench.

Judging by the expression on the depot owner's face, this wasn't going to be a fun conversation.

"What's up?"

Colt sighed. "I really don't know how to say this. I don't know where to start."

"At the beginning?"

"People keep telling me that," Colt mumbled. "Let me be clear. I don't want to do this, but she won't give me a moment's peace until I do."

"Anna?"

Colt looked to the side, shushed the air to his right, and then looked squarely at Tuck. "I see ghosts. Your grandmother is here."

# CHAPTER 4

Tuck blew right past the ghost part. "I don't have a grandmother. Never did." Growing up it had just been him and his parents, who'd both been pretty old when he'd been born. His dad's younger brother, Houston, the uncle who'd left him The Magnolia, hadn't come around much. There were no cousins. No grandparents. No family reunions.

Colt took a step closer. "You didn't know her, but of course you had a grandmother. Two, like everyone else, but I'm only dealing with the one." Again he looked to his right before returning his attention to Tuck. "You're the spitting image of your grandfather."

Tuck turned on his heel and walked away. If this was a joke, it was a cruel one. Years ago he'd accepted that when holidays rolled around he wouldn't have a family to share in the celebration. Now and then he'd spend Thanksgiving or Christmas with a friend and their family, but even though they were welcoming he always felt like an outsider looking in.

"When she saw you the other day she was struck by the resemblance, and then when you said your mother's name was Doreen..."

Tuck was about to walk into the public section of the depot, but he stopped short and spun around to face Colt. He might as well go back to the beginning himself. "Ghosts? Seriously? That's why you're always talking to yourself. It's..." Impossible. Ridiculous.

"I don't talk to myself, I talk to them." Colt looked and sounded stressed, as if he didn't like this any more than Tuck did. "I try not to, I promise you, but they won't leave me alone. Your grandmother Maude is one of the chattier ones. I haven't had a moment's peace since she saw you yesterday."

"Ghosts," Tuck said again. It shouldn't make sense, but in a twisted way it did. "Why should I believe you?"

"Why not?" Colt snapped.

*So many reasons...* "Let's say ghosts exist and you can see them. Why is this woman here? Why would Maude haunt you, of all people?"

"The *why me* is a long story. The *why here* is a bit simpler. Maude lived in the retirement home up the road. When she passed a couple of years ago, she gravitated here. Sad to say, she's not alone."

"I don't believe..."

Colt ignored him and continued. "She was engaged to your grandfather, Phillip Shelton. Maude's maiden name was..." Again that look to the right. "Reeves. A week before the wedding Phillip died. He was thrown from a horse and broke his neck. It was a couple of months before Maude realized she was pregnant with your mother. This was the fifties. Having the baby and raising her, a single mother, it just wasn't done. So Maude took a long vacation, had the baby, and then reluctantly agreed to put the child up for adoption. But not before she named her daughter Doreen."

"Nice tale," Tuck began, "but..."

"I suspect it's all verifiable." Again Colt looked to his right, but his eyes moved as if following Maude's ghost to Tuck's side. "No."

A warm breeze brushed Tuck's cheek, like a gentle wind on the beach. There was no breeze in the depot, and in December it wouldn't be warm even if there was.

"This is what's been holding her here," Colt said. "This secret, wondering what happened to Doreen, if she had a good life, if she had a family."

Tuck rushed past Colt, headed toward the back door. He didn't want to see anyone, and there were too damn many people in the record store. He was parked out back anyway, so it made sense to leave that way even if he wasn't in a panic. Nate Tucker didn't panic. Nothing touched him that deeply.

"She wants you to have…" Colt called out as Tuck pushed the rear door open on a couple of cars, Colt's battered truck, a dumpster, and Tuck's Ford.

He didn't care what a ghost wanted him to have.

Until this moment his holiday wish had been simple. A dance with a pretty girl who said she didn't dance. Now what he really wanted for Christmas was not to know what he'd just been told. A grandmother, right around the corner all these years. A blood relative within reach for *years* and he'd had no idea.

He wanted to forget, but most of all he just wanted to be alone. Alone, as he'd always been and would always be.

∽

IT WAS another busy day in Dawn's Radiance. Olive wasn't as easily annoyed by difficult customers today. She was sure her improved mood had nothing to do with Tuck, but she did keep looking at the door, wondering when he'd come in to pick up his scarves.

She liked him, more than a little. She'd never admit that out loud, but he was hot and had a great smile and bought extravagant gifts for old ladies who might not otherwise get anything at all for Christmas. Why on earth had no one snatched him up by now? Really great guys weren't single for long. In her experience great, single guys were all too rare.

Closing time came and went, and still no Tuck. He must've gotten busy, either with his business or something to do with the volunteer fire department. He *did* have a life, she was sure. There might've been a fire, or some other emergency that called out the firefighters.

Olive gathered her purse and light jacket, then put all of Tuck's small bags with the carefully folded scarves into one big bag for the walk home. Not home, not really, but like it or not the blue house was beginning to feel a *little* like an actual home. At least for now.

She'd deliver the scarves to Tuck, if he was home, eat her leftover shrimp and grits for supper, then head to Dawn's to check on the very pregnant woman and her family. It was a plan. She'd sleep well tonight, for sure. Running a business was exhausting! If she'd decided to stay with Dawn and her family it would be even more so. A handsome neighbor who liked to flirt was a nice distraction.

He really wasn't her type at all. Did she have a type? If she did, Tuck wasn't it. He was an easygoing, bar-owning volunteer fireman who had no noticeable regular schedule. Sometimes he was at The Magnolia, other times he was not. He came and went as he pleased, as if he didn't have a care in the world. She, on the other hand, scheduled her day from that first cup of coffee to the moment she crawled into bed.

His two-story white house waited just ahead, impossible to miss. Her little blue cottage sat beyond, almost hidden from this vantage point. She could walk past, go home, kick off her shoes, maybe drop the bag of scarves on his porch later, like a coward.

No, she would not be cowardly. Olive turned on the walkway between the sidewalk and Tuck's house, then took quick steps up the three stairs to his front porch. His truck was in the driveway, so she assumed he was home. Unless he'd walked somewhere, which was always possible. She did love that Seawolf Beach was such a walkable town. At home, her *real* home, she couldn't go anywhere without battling traffic.

She knocked. When there was no response, she punched the doorbell. It was a big house, much bigger than her own. He could be upstairs, in the rear of the house, maybe even in the backyard. The doorbell tone echoed through the house. She'd decided Tuck wasn't at home and was thinking of leaving a note when the door swung open.

For a moment, she couldn't speak. Tuck didn't look, well, like Tuck. No easy smile, no twinkle in those blue eyes. He was pale and haggard. "What's wrong?" she asked.

"What makes you think anything's wrong?"

*The way you look. The sound of your voice. The clear tension in that combative stance.* "Call it a hunch."

"I've had a bad day, that's all. Are those the scarves? Sorry, I forgot all about them." He reached out and took the bag she offered. "I'll drop them at the fire station tomorrow."

She should turn away, leave him to his misery, and continue with her plans for the day. Leftover shrimp and grits. A visit with Dawn. But something stopped her. "Let me make you dinner," she said before she could stop herself.

His eyebrows arched a little. "Really?"

"Nothing fancy." The leftovers could wait. "I make a mean omelet." That was all she had the makings for, at the moment.

He started to say no; she saw that *no* on his face. But after a short pause he said, "It would do me good to get out of the house. Thanks."

"Give me twenty minutes," Olive said, intent on a quick shower before she started cooking. "I have retail smell all over me."

Finally, he smiled. That grin wasn't as bright as usual, but it was a definite improvement.

Olive didn't run to her own house, but she did hurry. She could call Dawn later and check on her instead of visiting tonight. Tomorrow would be soon enough for a face-to-face chat. As she let herself into the blue house, the Christmas tree caught her eye. This morning before she'd headed out, she'd unplugged the lights. It wasn't safe to leave anything plugged in, that's what she told herself.

She dropped her purse in a chair and walked straight to the tree, leaned over, grabbed the cord, and plugged it into the outlet. She didn't need or want a Christmas tree but since it was here, she might as well enjoy the lights. They were festive, which would've normally been a negative in her book.

Why had she invited Tuck over? Simple. They were neighbors, *friends*, and when he'd opened the door he'd looked like a man who needed a friend tonight.

As she walked toward the bedroom to grab clean clothes, she muttered to herself. "Liar. You *like* him."

# CHAPTER 5

Tuck knocked on Olive's door right on time. He could've hidden away and sulked for the evening, maybe for the next few days, but when she'd invited him for dinner he'd been so surprised he'd been compelled to accept. A spur-of-the-moment invitation wasn't like her. At least, it wasn't like the woman he'd thought her to be. Not that he was complaining. He wasn't sure what to expect, but his temporary next-door neighbor had a way of taking his mind off everything else.

She answered the door quickly, unlike him. In his defense when she'd rung his doorbell, he hadn't known it was her...

She'd slipped into something more comfortable for the evening, which wasn't as exciting as it was in the movies. Baggy sweatpants and an oversized Seawolf Beach T-shirt did not make for a seductive outfit. Olive's dark hair was still damp from the shower. She'd scrubbed her face clean. She was gorgeous.

In a matter of days she'd surprised him in so many ways. He hadn't seen her coming.

He stood in the kitchen doorway and watched as she cooked. She made the huge omelet as if it wasn't the first time. No bacon, more's the pity, but she did have toast and jam to go with the cheese omelet she slid from the pan, cut in half, and then placed on the kitchen table. Coffee was already made.

Their conversation could be awkward, he supposed. They didn't know one another all that well, and at the same time... they did. They talked about customers between bites, commiserating over the challenging ones and laughing at those who deserved to be laughed at. There were good stories, too. Little kids shopping for a parent or grandparent. Women shopping for friends and being thrilled to find just the right gift. Tuck even talked about a few of his regular customers, and the local bands who performed at The Magnolia on a regular basis.

It was a pleasant conversation, and Olive was definitely pleasant to look at. He could almost forget what Colt had told him, could *almost* write the entire Maude story off as a ridiculous fantasy. But he hadn't imagined that warm breeze on one cheek, or the gut instinct that told him it was all true.

One of these days he'd sit down at the computer and do a search on Maude Reeves and Phillip Shelton. But not today. In truth, he didn't really want to know. The idea that he might've had a grandmother living right around the corner all these years gutted him. She'd been *right there,* but the news of her existence had come too late. He didn't do broken hearts but hearing the truth, if it was the truth, broke his heart a little.

Olive made things better. He could've called one of his guy friends if he wanted a night out, but how on earth could he explain? Beyond a simple "what's wrong?" Olive hadn't asked for explanations.

They sat on the couch after supper, staring at her little Christmas tree decorated with white lights and a few plain gold ornaments. No tinsel or garland, no personal touches. She had a cup of herbal tea in her hands; he held a mug of coffee. It was cozy. Nice. Friendly.

He wanted more than friendship from her, but now, while he

was reeling, was probably not the time to make a move. What an oddly mature and unexpected thought.

He could easily lose himself in Olive, if she'd have him. A kiss, a well-placed hand, skin-to-skin contact of any kind would soothe him. He didn't go there. After they talked about customers and bands they turned to a discussion of Dawn and Mike, their kids, other volunteer firefighters and their annual gift drive. During a pause in the conversation, while Olive was taking a sip of tea, Tuck asked, "Do you believe in ghosts?"

He'd suspected she might spit tea and laugh at him, but she did neither. "I haven't had any ghostly experiences, but I know people who have. Or say they have. Anything is possible, right? I can't say there are no mysteries in the universe." She looked at him then, square on. "Why do you ask?"

Colt hadn't explicitly said his ability was a secret, but it was implied, right? If he wanted everyone to know, he would've told the world years ago.

"I have a friend who says he sees ghosts, and I wondered... Is he crazy? Delusional? Or maybe..."

"The guy at the record store? Colt?"

So much for keeping a secret. Maybe it wasn't a secret after all. "Could be. How did you know?"

"I didn't *know*, not really, but I have seen the way he talks to himself, and Dawn said there was a rumor the depot was haunted. Since the man who owns it walks around talking to air, or maybe to people no one else can see if you believe in that kind of thing, it isn't much of a leap."

Felt like a damn long leap to him. "I've always been a believer of what I can see with my own eyes and not much else."

"Most of us are," Olive said. "Colt could be off his rocker, but maybe he has an ability the rest of us will never understand. I'd like to think there are still secrets in the world, that we haven't figured everything out just yet. A little mystery is a good thing."

She laughed. "I can't believe I said that. I can't stand not knowing everything, but maybe when it comes to ghosts I can let that slide."

"I kinda like having everything figured out." Talking to Olive had eased his mind. Nothing had changed, he didn't know where to go from here, but his heart no longer raced and his thoughts had calmed. The news Colt had shared called for investigation; he had to know if what he'd said, through Maude, was the truth. But he didn't have to start anything tonight. "I confess, I don't quite have you figured out."

Leaning in and over to kiss her was instinct. Not planned, not thought through. He surprised her, but she kissed him back. They each still held a mug in their hands. He stopped kissing her long enough to put his mug on the coffee table, then he took her herbal tea and placed it there, too. She didn't protest.

When their hands were free, she swayed into him, not away. Her warmth and softness were a pleasure, ones that made him forget for a moment that his world had been turned upside down. She draped an arm around his neck, pulled him closer, deepened the kiss.

It would be so easy to lose himself in her. Too easy. He felt himself falling, falling, getting more lost in her with every second that passed. The kiss was amazing, but he wanted so much more than a kiss. He wanted all of her. Bare from head to toe, wrapped around him, needing him the way he needed her. That could happen right here on this couch, which was surprisingly roomy. In her bed. In his bed. He didn't care where.

*Whoa. Too fast.* One kiss did not a relationship make, and he was too damn old for one-night stands that were always a disappointment. Besides, Olive wasn't a one-night stand woman. She deserved more. She deserved better.

Sleeping with her so soon, so impulsively, would destroy whatever friendship they were forming. If he didn't stop kissing her, that one last rational thought would fade to nothing in a heartbeat. It wouldn't be fair to bury his anger and fear by burying himself in her. She might be the right woman, but this was the wrong time.

Maybe she had the same thought, because before he could back away, she did. She didn't look upset or surprised. He didn't see regret in her dark brown eyes.

"I needed that," she said softly.

"Me, too."

"I haven't been surprised for a very long time."

She didn't say what had surprised her. The kiss, probably, but maybe it was more.

"I've had my own share of surprises today," he confessed.

"Care to share?"

"Let's just say the other surprise wasn't nearly as pleasant as you."

She smiled, and he almost moved in again. Olive was a tempting woman. It had been a long time since he'd been so intrigued. Right now, when he was wondering who the hell he really was, probably wasn't the time to give in to temptation.

"I should go," he said, but he didn't stand.

"Yes, you should." She didn't move, either.

"If I don't..."

Olive sighed, and then she looked at the Christmas tree. Avoiding him in some small way? Maybe. Still, neither of them moved. "I didn't expect... anything like this. I'm really not in the market for a relationship."

"Neither am I."

"But we can be friends, right?"

Tuck stood slowly. "Sure. I need to go." *While I still can...*

"I hope you feel better."

Standing by the couch, he looked down at her. "I do." He'd forgotten about ghosts and grandmothers and lost opportunities for a while. "Thanks, friend." He headed for the door, turned to look back at her. "Do you have plans for Sunday?"

"No. Unless you count sleeping in as a plan. That's the one day the boutique is closed."

He'd been thinking of asking her to spend Sunday with him, but when she mentioned sleeping in, he changed his mind. "Go out with me Saturday night. Dinner. Dancing." And who knows what else...

"No dancing," she said. "But dinner would be lovely."

He grinned at her. "Great. Wear something sexy."

∽

OLIVE STARED at the closed door. Wear something sexy? She didn't own anything sexy! And if she did, she wouldn't have brought it with her. She'd packed clothes for working at the boutique and for exercise. One red and green T-shirt with a holiday themed gnome on it for the family gathering, since south Mississippi was too warm for her ugly Christmas sweater. All her shoes were comfortable, made for standing or walking. All the clothes she'd packed were *practical*.

Of course, she *did* work at a boutique that had a few sexy offerings.

When she'd come here to help Dawn she hadn't imagined her stay might include a date that wasn't really a date and a hot neighbor who kissed as if there was nothing and no one else in the world. How could she have prepared herself for Tuck?

Maybe nothing would come of it. They didn't have all that much in common, she had to admit. Again, she wasn't looking for a man, and if she was... he wasn't her type. She told herself that again and again.

But really, did she even have a type? Hot, kind, and chivalrous should be every woman's type. And that kiss...

It was going to take some time to wind down after that. She wasn't in the mood for TV and didn't want to pick up her book. Her mind reeled with the wonderfulness of reality; she wasn't interested in fiction at the moment.

Olive grabbed her phone and pulled up a favorite album from her music app. She listened, lost in the lyrics and the flow of the notes while she did a few stretches to work out the kinks brought on by a long day on her feet. She closed her eyes, stretched her arms over her head, twisted side to side. It felt good. She bent down to touch her toes and swept back up again. And again. She balanced on one foot, a yoga pose she'd learned in a class she'd started last year.

The second song on the album was a slow, pleasant, almost generic pop tune. She let the music wash over her as she moved. She didn't think about Tuck for a few long seconds. She didn't give a moment of brain power to retail or family or Christmas. Instead she simply felt the music. Her stretching turned into a dance of sorts as she moved. Up, down, around, a twist. And there was Tuck again, creeping into her thoughts.

*Dinner and dancing* he'd said. And oh, that *kiss*.

In the middle of the song, she stopped moving and forced herself to stand perfectly still. What the hell was happening to her? Nothing and no one made her dance. Not even Nathaniel Tucker.

# CHAPTER 6

Thursday at Dawn's Radiance was a little too slow for Olive's liking. There were fewer customers than usual, and the ones who did come in were efficient, in and out, giving her nothing to complain about.

Rearranging clothing and doodads only took so much time and effort, so she did a little shopping of her own. *Wear something sexy.* She should be perverse and dress in her Christmas gnome T-shirt, sweats, and tennis shoes for their date, but the idea of dressing up for Tuck was appealing. She set aside a slinky red dress and tried on a couple pairs of shoes before settling on the black heels. They'd go with pretty much anything, she reasoned. She plucked a pair of dangly earrings from a rack by the checkout counter, and then placed a very pretty, sparkly evening bag behind the counter.

Why was she going to so much trouble for a *friend*? Kiss or not, that's all Tuck was, all he could ever be. Still, there was nothing wrong with putting in a little extra effort to look spectacular for the first date she'd been on in... years. Holy cow, had it been that long?

She carried her purchases in an oversized shopping bag, as

she walked home. On the way she passed a couple of women she recognized from the boutique. They'd been so familiar with the store, so comfortable in the space, they had to be regular customers. They smiled and waved and she did the same as best she could with her hands full. Small-town living was a new experience for her. She didn't want to like it so much, but she did.

Her leftover shrimp and grits made for a great supper, but to be honest they'd been much better with Tuck sitting on the other side of the table. There was just something about that man. The way he smiled, the twinkle in his eyes. Maybe he was a player, maybe he made every woman feel as if she were the only one in the room, in the *world*...

The truth was, reheated shrimp and grits tasted just as good as they had right out of Maggie's kitchen, but she missed the company.

Tuck's gray truck wasn't parked in the driveway. She checked more than once from the side window, the one behind her little Christmas tree. He *did* have a life, she conceded. A business. Other friends. She shouldn't care, shouldn't even bother to peer out the window. As she'd told him plainly, she wasn't looking for a relationship.

Olive went to bed disappointed that Tuck wasn't at home, in his own bed, next door where he belonged. She slept deeply; she dreamed and woke a little late to the tail end of a dream she couldn't quite remember, even though she wanted to. She was pretty sure she'd dreamed about her neighbor.

She should've enjoyed her slow Thursday instead of complaining, because on Friday she arrived to a couple of customers, friends judging by the way they talked, waiting for her to open. It wasn't yet ten but she let them in to browse while she got set up. Dawn called just after opening time to ask her to stop by that evening and to bring the books. Olive made a note to make sure the accounting ledger was up-to-date. Who didn't use computer software for this kind of thing? Her sister, that's who.

The day was a blur of happy and/or stressed customers. There were less than two weeks until Christmas. Shoppers were running out of time. Olive was happy to help them find just the right gift. It kept her mind off Tuck, sexy dresses, and unexpected kisses.

She hadn't been involved with a man for years. Romance was too messy, and yes, she was still wary of all men after her experience with Stefan. Friends had set her up a time or two, or tried to, but those awkward meetings for coffee or maybe the occasional actual date never went anywhere. How could they, when she started off every relationship wondering how and when these men would disappoint her?

Whatever this was with Tuck didn't have to go anywhere, either. How could it? He had a life here; she had a life in Birmingham. Just because they'd hit it off didn't mean whatever this was had to be serious. She could enjoy his company for a couple of weeks, date, maybe even...

Yes, *maybe even*. It had been a long time.

Anna stopped by after lunch. Olive wouldn't drive any customer away, but... why was Anna here? The few times she'd seen Colt's fiancée, Anna had been casually dressed. Jeans, T-shirts, tennis shoes. She looked great in them, but other than the jeans that hung on a rack in the back, nothing here was Anna's style.

Maybe Colt had asked her to *wear something sexy*.

"Can I help you find anything?" Olive asked as Anna looked through a rack of silky blouses that were not her style and were also *not* sexy.

"I'm doing a little Christmas shopping. My mother loves this boutique, so it's a great place to start."

Olive smiled. That made sense. She couldn't see Anna wearing any of those frou-frou blouses.

Why did so many people wait until December to do their shopping? She'd bought and wrapped gifts for her parents, Dawn and Mike, and the girls in September.

Should she get something for Tuck? That thought came and went. No. He was a friendly neighbor and a good kisser, nothing more. Just because he managed to take her mind off her worries, old and new, that didn't mean she had to buy him a Christmas present. They didn't have that kind of relationship. Shoot, they didn't have a *relationship* at all!

Anna chose a colorful blouse, then went back for another. As she placed them on the counter, she sighed. "Mom doesn't need another thing, but believe it or not she's dating one of my aunt's neighbors, and she sure thinks she needs new clothes. She'll be here for Christmas, just for a few days. Her boyfriend is driving her." Anna cut her eyes up. "They're staying at a B and B up the road. I'm sure she'd come by and spend a small fortune, but I think y'all will be closed while she's here."

Olive smiled. "I'll open up for her, if I'm still around while she's in town. Sounds like she's a good customer."

"She used to be, that's for sure."

Anna took a deep breath and looked Olive in the eye. There was an uncertainty in that expression, a reluctance, before she said, "I hear you're dating Tuck."

A warm flush heated Olive's cheeks. Small towns! They had their charm, and their disadvantages. "I wouldn't say *dating*, exactly." Not yet, anyway. "We're just friendly neighbors." For now.

"Oh. I thought maybe..." Anna shrugged her shoulders.

"Wait a minute," Olive said. "Did you come here to warn me about something to do with Tuck? Is there anything I need to know?"

Anna smiled. "No. He's a great guy who could, frankly, use a good woman in his life. Colt's been trying to get up with him, and he isn't returning calls or answering texts."

That didn't sound like Tuck, not to her. "I think he's been busy with his business. I haven't seen him around for a couple of days."

Anna took her shopping bag, smiled, wished Olive a Merry Christmas, and left.

Thank goodness the rest of the day stayed busy. It didn't give Olive much time to wonder what the hell was going on with her next-door neighbor.

But in those quiet moments while she was alone in the boutique, she did wonder...

~

It was easy enough to lose himself in work. There was always something to be done at The Magnolia. In the past two days he'd reorganized the back room and taken care of some touch-up painting in the main area. He'd reconfigured his spreadsheets and then put them back into the original format again, which had been a complete waste of time. He needed to waste time to keep himself from thinking too much.

Colt had called several times, or tried to. He'd left a couple of messages Tuck had opted not to respond to. The texts had been deleted unread. Colt's number was now silenced. Couldn't the man understand that Tuck needed time to think?

On a Friday night, The Magnolia was packed. The music hadn't started yet, but the band, a popular local group, was setting up on the stage. Music brought in the customers and he had to admit, he could get lost in the right songs himself. A good Friday-night crowd meant he could help Ginny at the bar, which was another way to lose himself in something besides family secrets and grandmothers. This was a job he could do with his eyes closed. No deep thoughts required.

He served a beer to a regular customer, turned around, and there she was, walking through his door.

Olive looked woefully out of place in The Magnolia, as if she'd wandered in from another world. She truly was from another world, or might as well be. She came from a decent family who loved each other. She'd grown up with and still had Christmases and birthday celebrations, the constant of family. Parents, a sister, nieces... grandmothers. She was not like him.

Damn, she was sexy as hell, and she didn't seem to know it. Several pairs of eyes followed her progress through the room, to the bar where he waited for her. What was that feeling that welled up in him? Couldn't be jealousy. Couldn't be possessiveness.

So why was he so sure, as she sat on a stool before him, that she was his?

Ridiculous. He barely knew her; she was just a way to escape from reality for a while. Any beautiful woman who kissed like Olive would elicit the same feelings, the same sense of connection. He didn't have time for this, didn't want to lean on her or anyone else.

"I heard that someone here makes a mean burger," she said.

"Slumming it?" he asked, more harshly than he'd intended.

She looked surprised, maybe a little hurt, but she quickly let it go. "I need to get my car out and drive it now and then. And I'm hungry. Dawn said I could eat at her house, but it was just too much. The girls. The dogs. Her in-laws."

"It's a lot," Tuck said. He'd been at Mike's house before, several times, and had the same thought. *Too much.*

"After a week of retail I could use a glass of wine with my burger. I've earned it."

"Red or white?"

"Red. Do you have…"

"I have this." He reached beneath the bar and grabbed a can.

Olive's eyes widened; not in a good way. "Your wine comes in a *can*?"

"I'll put it in a glass for you, princess." He grabbed a wine glass, put it on the bar, opened the can, and poured.

She might've taken offense at the term *princess,* but all she did was wrinkle her nose in his direction before taking a sip of her red wine. He wasn't sure if the drink met with her approval or not, but after that first sip she didn't push the glass back toward him.

He went to the kitchen to put in her order, then placed himself before her again.

What was she doing here? How had she slipped her way into his life? Olive was tempting, he had to admit. Tempting enough to take his mind off the news Colt had shared, as well as the busy holiday season that seemed to be exploding around him. She was his neighbor, for a while. A friend, or getting there. More than a friend?

Maybe.

She spun on her stool and looked around the place. "So, this is the infamous Magnolia."

"It is. Not as infamous as it was when my uncle ran it, but…" He shrugged his shoulders. "Probably not the best place for a woman like you to come on her own."

"A woman like me?"

"A nice girl." Not just nice, naive. Gullible. Why on earth had he ever thought… wished… dreamed… that she might end up in his bed?

"It doesn't seem that bad," she said.

"It's still early," he countered. "Give it a little time."

She didn't let it go. Did she ever let anything go? "If it's such a terrible place, why are you here?"

He'd asked himself that same question, more than once. The answer was always the same. "Imperfect as it is, this is my place in the world." His world, not hers. He needed to remember that.

"Your place can be wherever you want it to be," she said.

She was definitely naive. Clueless? No, he wouldn't go that far.

Olive's meal came out of the kitchen in a basket, loaded with fries and an oversized burger. She glanced down at it and laughed. "I can't eat all this!" She looked up, with those deep, dark brown eyes of hers. "Have you eaten? Want half?"

"You keep feeding me."

"You fed me. Seems only fair."

"I can get you a to-go box for the leftovers."

"Leftover fries and burgers are never good." She took the plastic knife that was tucked into her basket and cut the burger in half. Without asking she grabbed a napkin, placed it before him, and carefully deposited the half burger.

"I can't eat while I'm back here," he argued.

She slid the napkin and burger to the side and patted the stool beside her.

Damn, she was persistent.

Tuck rounded the bar and took the stool next to Olive's. He gestured for Ginny to grab another can of wine and bring him a beer. His bartender seemed amused by the situation. She got a glare for her trouble, but didn't seem to mind.

"It is a good burger," Olive said as she slid the basket closer to him. "Eat some of the fries. They're great, but there's no way I can eat this much."

He grabbed a fry and popped it into his mouth. As the salt hit his tongue, he realized that he hadn't eaten since a sandwich last night. His mind had been on everything but food.

"Tell me about this uncle of yours," she said.

"Why?"

"You're here, keeping his legacy alive. He must've been important to you."

Might as well let her know what she was getting into... "Houston Tucker was an enormous shithead."

Olive looked down at her fries and muttered, "Oh."

"Don't get me wrong. He did take me in after Mom died. I was thirteen, and soon after I moved in with him I was headed for all kinds of trouble. Yes, he was a shithead, but he was the only family I had and I was the same for him."

"You've been here since the age of thirteen?"

Was that a touch of horror in her voice? Maybe he imagined that reaction. Why would she care?

Tuck shook his head. "Yep. I joined the Army at eighteen, as soon as I could. I couldn't wait to get out of town, away from Uncle Houston, on to something else. Anything else."

"I don't get military vibes from you, not at all," Olive said.

"Yeah, I'm not a fan of taking orders. I knew early on that I wouldn't make a career of it, but I did my time as best I could, learned a lot, made a handful of lifelong friends. When I was done with that, I headed to Florida."

"You were Florida Man." She sent a wide, charming smile in his direction.

He had to grin at that. "For a while. I got a job as a bouncer in a bar in the Keys. I liked it, the place and the job." He still thought about that time in his life, now and then. More than once he'd considered leaving all this behind and going back to a simpler life.

"If you liked it so much, why did you leave?"

Ah, the truth. Might as well tell all. "Uncle Houston got sick, and I came home to take care of him." That hadn't been a happy time in his life. Three years of taking care of a man who didn't want anyone else to know he was sick. A man who didn't like his nephew all that much. A man who was the only family Tuck had in the world.

Except...

He shouldn't have kept his back to the room for this long, not on a Friday night. Introspection was interrupted by a shout, a scream, the sound of something heavy hitting the floor.

Tuck spun around and leapt off the stool. The fight wasn't more than six feet away, and the drunken combatants were making their way toward Olive.

## CHAPTER 7

Olive squealed and closed her eyes. As if that would help. She had nowhere to go! The polished wooden bar was behind her. Directly before her two older men wrestled beer belly to beer belly, edging closer and closer to her, cursing at each other. It was difficult to understand everything they said, but the contentious subject seemed to be football, of all things. She opened one eye; they weren't more than a foot away. The jabs they threw were ineffective, for the most part, but they did throw them, one after another. One meaty fist came much too close to her shoulder.

Tuck thrust himself between the two men and separated them easily, one hand fisted on a T-shirt, the other gripping a collar. He pushed them back and away from her. The fighters were separated, then with a move she couldn't quite explain, Tuck put them each, one at a time, on their asses. He stood over them prepared to do whatever was necessary to keep them down.

His efficiency and chivalry were both incredibly hot. *Oh my.*

"Don't make me call Mac," he said in a firm voice. "I will, if you both don't get out of here, now. You've had enough to drink tonight. Go home and sleep it off." As the men awkwardly rose to their feet and stumbled toward the exit, Tuck added, in a raised voice, "If you fight in the parking lot, you'll both be banned from The Magnolia for six months!"

One of the men looked back, eyes widened in surprise. "You would never do such a thing. We're your best customers."

"Not when you upset the pretty lady," Tuck said with a wave of his hand in her direction.

One of the men stumbled and all but fell out the door. The other was right behind but stopped to call out, "Sorry, pretty lady."

The excitement had begun and ended pretty quickly, but Olive's heart pounded double time. Tuck placed himself between her and the rest of the crowd, who all watched. Since the brawlers were gone the entertainment was over, there was no one to watch but Tuck, and her.

"Are you okay?"

Olive nodded her head, but couldn't find her voice.

"Are you sure?" He looked down the bar. "Ginny, get Olive another can of wine."

Her initial response to that was a brief, sharp burst of laughter. Another *can* of wine! "No, no, if I have any more, I won't be able to drive. I'm a lightweight. If I drink any more, I'll need a designated driver."

"You're looking at one," he said.

"I need to go to the grocery store on the way home..."

"I'll take you to the grocery store, if it can't wait."

He had an argument for everything. "Who's Mac?" she asked.

"Chief of police. He's even better than I am at breaking up bar fights, and everyone's more afraid of him than they are of me."

"No one should be afraid of you." She sure wasn't. "You're not scary at all."

"Get into a fight in my bar and maybe you'll think differently." That statement was followed by a smile. He did have a *very* charming smile.

Her mind continued to spin and her heart beat too fast. More wine might not have been the best cure for either, but she took it anyway.

"How many cans of wine would it take to get you on the dance floor?" Tuck asked in a lowered voice.

"More than I'm going to drink, tonight or ever."

"Too bad."

He sat beside her and took a bite of his half of the burger, but she'd lost her appetite so what was left of her half sat, untouched.

The band played their first song, one she recognized but couldn't name. Something from the seventies, she thought. It was nice. Her toes wiggled a little and her butt squirmed, but she remained steadfast in her refusal to dance.

Halfway through her third glass of wine, she realized how lightheaded she'd become. Her mind wandered all over the place. That fist that had come so close. Tuck coming to her rescue. The new, sexy dress that was hanging in her closet. Her knight in shining armor stayed right beside her, as if he was worried. Worried about her. That was sweet, but unnecessary. She could and would take care of herself.

Though the two pot-bellied men would've been a challenge if they'd moved any closer.

She spun on her stool to face Tuck. "You're still a bouncer, aren't you?"

"Some nights I am."

"What else do you do?" Besides fight fires and shop for old ladies and break up bar fights and flirt with neighbors.

"I do pretty much everything around here. Cleaning, bartending, cooking if I have to, accounting. I've married a few people, too."

Oh, no. "How many times have you been married?" she asked, her voice squeaking a little on that final word.

He grinned at her. *Oh, that smile.* "I worded that badly. Sorry. I'm ordained in the Sacred Ministry of Eternal Union. You'd be surprised how many people want to tie the knot under a neon beer sign."

That was a relief. At least he wasn't a serial husband. "Jack of all trades…"

"Master of none?" he finished.

"I didn't say that. You seem to do everything well." Even… Nope, not going there. Lots of men were good kissers. No need to offer praise in that department. Wine made her too talkative. Always. "I bought something sexy for our date tomorrow night."

"Did you?"

"Yes. You did ask me to, and I complied. It's red. I look good in red."

"I'm sure you do."

"I haven't been on a date in ages," she whispered. "I haven't been…" She stopped. Thank goodness she wasn't far enough gone to finish that sentence.

"You haven't been…" he prodded.

"I haven't been this tipsy in a long time." She pushed what was left of her third glass, which wasn't much, away. "I'll definitely need a driver tonight."

That's not all she needed.

∽

A SLIGHTLY DRUNKEN Olive had taken his mind off everything. Between the fight, keeping her safe, the way she looked at him sometimes... He hadn't thought about ghosts and grandmothers until he remembered that he hadn't thought about them for a while.

Olive probably didn't know how cute she was when she was tipsy; she might hit him if he told her.

That *I haven't been...* stayed on his mind as he drove her home. *I haven't been tempted. I haven't been laid. I haven't been...*

As he steered the truck onto Jasmine Street, she started to sing. "Jingle Bells." Maybe she could dance, or at least she'd once been able to, but she couldn't carry a tune. At least, not in her current condition. She looked out the window, studying the lights and other decorations as they drove slowly past.

"I should like Christmas again by now, don't you think?" she asked as he pulled into his driveway.

"I don't know. Should you?"

"Maybe. I mean, until I was dropped in front of hundreds of people and my career as a dancer ended with a crack, I loved the holidays. The music, the presents, the decorations. The food! Oh, my mom makes the best spice cake, but only for Christmas."

"Do you still eat it?"

"Duh, yes. Maybe I hate Christmas but I'm not a glutton for punishment."

Hate was a strong word. He wondered if she meant that, truly. Now was not the time to ask. "So you just don't like the music and the decorations."

"I don't like the constant reminder that I'm no longer who I was meant to be."

He rounded the truck and opened her door, then helped her down. She was still a little wobbly. "Maybe you were wrong about what you were meant to be."

She ignored him. "You're good at taking care of people in so many ways. I see that, even if you don't. You took care of Uncle

Shithead, you took care of me when I thought I was going to be bowled over by two fat guys, and you bought nice, expensive scarves for old ladies! You fight fires, and that's another way of being a caretaker. You make dreams come true by marrying couples under beer neon. You can do anything, I bet, anything you want. If you wanted to be an EMT, or a nurse, or even a doctor, you could do it. You have that option. I will *never* be a prima ballerina. I will *never* dance onstage again, I will *never*..."

"Maybe you should focus on what you can do instead of what you can't."

She didn't immediately respond as they walked up the steps to her front porch. Olive opened her purse, reached inside, and fumbled for her keys. With the key ring in hand, she turned to him. "That's not an entirely terrible idea. I suppose I should get over being dropped by a man I thought..." There was a short pause before she rose up on her toes and kissed him. Not a sweet little thank you peck on the lips, no, this was a warm, arousing, tempting kiss. Those lips. That tongue.

She was too drunk for him to do anything about it. Tempted as he was, he wouldn't be *that guy*.

The kiss ended and she took one step back. He asked, "Why did you do that?"

She smiled at him. "Because I can." She unlocked the door and opened it. "I would ask you in, but... I can't. I'm going to put on my pajamas and have some ice cream to sober up, then I'll get a good night's sleep."

"Ice cream?"

"Works every time," she said as she stepped inside. "Not that I need sobering often, but Jessica, my business partner, she likes wine with dinner and she holds hers much better than I hold mine, so when we have occasion to celebrate... which isn't at all important." She looked him in the eye. "Thank you for bringing me home. I guess I'll see you tomorrow."

"Six o'clock," he said. He couldn't wait to see her in her sexy red dress...

# CHAPTER 8

More than one glass of wine wasn't a good thing. At least, not for her. Whether it started in a can or a bottle, she needed to be more careful. Thinking back on last night...

She hadn't made any huge mistakes, and she hadn't been so far gone that she couldn't remember what had happened, but still, she'd probably said a few things she shouldn't have.

Olive was doubly thankful that Saturday was a short day at Dawn's Radiance. The regular customers were aware of the hours, so the morning was busy enough that she only thought about her upcoming date a time or two. Maybe ten. The red dress hung in her closet, waiting. The shoes were magnificent. She did hope Tuck didn't expect her to walk far to wherever they were going for dinner.

Time to be honest with herself. She didn't give a fig about dinner. She hadn't felt this way about a man in a very long time. Her time in Seawolf Beach would be short, and she didn't want to waste a single day. She wasn't looking for a permanent guy, a real relationship, a forever love. But that didn't mean she should waste her time here, ignore whatever this was with Tuck. He was unexpected, a surprise of sorts. A Christmas surprise?

The matter was decided. She was going to sleep with Nathaniel Tucker. Tonight.

As if he knew she was thinking about him, he walked in five minutes before closing time. Shoppers had cleared out, leaving her alone to handle a few bookkeeping details before locking up. He smiled. Her stomach knotted. *Tonight.*

"I thought I'd run you to The Magnolia to pick up your car as soon as you're done here."

"Thanks. Almost ready."

He nodded, then browsed a shelf of creams and lotions while she took care of end-of-day paperwork and storing the bank bag of cash in the back room safe. Most people charged their purchases, but a few paid with cash and she had to keep an appropriate amount of change on hand. Monday she needed to make a trip to the bank before opening the shop.

She didn't want to think about Monday, banking, or customers. Tuck was on her mind. Boy, was he.

His truck was parked at the curb. She locked up. He opened the passenger door for her and held her hand while she stepped up and in, and they were on their way. He didn't talk much during the short drive and neither did she. When they pulled into the parking lot of his bar, she wondered if she'd wasted an opportunity. She wasn't going to be here long. She needed to make the best of whatever time she had with Tuck.

Half an hour after leaving the boutique, she parked in her driveway. Tuck, who'd been right behind her, pulled into his. She had a few hours to get ready for their date, more than enough time, so when he headed her way she didn't protest.

"Got any coffee?" he asked.

"Always."

"Make me a cup?"

"Sure. I could use one myself." And maybe a cookie.

"Sold," he said with a charming grin.

Was she an idiot, falling for that grin? Maybe. She didn't really care.

Olive kicked off her shoes, dropped her purse in an empty chair, and headed toward the kitchen. Pod coffee and store-bought Christmas cookies were hardly gourmet, but they'd do. Tuck stood in the kitchen doorway and watched her. He looked better than he had the last couple of days, less stressed. More himself. Whatever had upset him had been resolved or forgotten.

He took the cookies into the living room and placed them on the coffee table. When she walked into the room with two mugs of coffee, the lights on her tree were twinkling. He'd turned them on. She didn't mind at all.

She handed him a coffee cup and sat beside him. He'd kissed her here, on this couch, a few days ago. If she was smart she'd move her purse and sit in the chair, to avoid temptation. Where Tuck was concerned she wasn't smart. Not at all.

"Where are we going for dinner tonight?" she asked.

"There's a really great seafood restaurant in Biloxi. I made reservations."

"It'll have to go a long way to beat Maggie's," she said, then she placed her half-empty coffee mug on the coffee table by the cookies she had no appetite for, at the moment.

"Trust me," Tuck said.

Did she trust him? Yeah, she did. "I'm sorry if I was... difficult last night."

"Difficult?"

"Okay, woozy. I overindulged. I was kinda drunk."

"Kinda?"

"Fine. I was a lightweight wino who criticized your wine containers and then drank too much. You had to drive me home when I'm sure you had other things to do."

"None of them would've been as fun as spending a little more time with you."

That was a nice thing to say, but was he honest or full of shit? Was he spinning a tale so she'd sleep with him? Should she tell him he didn't have to work so hard? Of course not. She'd lose her woman card if she did. Maybe he didn't need to work too hard for her, but that didn't mean she wanted him to think she was easy.

"You're a good neighbor and a good friend."

He placed his coffee cup beside hers, leaned in, and kissed her. Last time he'd kissed her on the couch it had been amazing, but they were closer now than they'd been then and she knew without a doubt that she wanted him. For today, for tomorrow, while she was in Seawolf Beach... a hunk for Christmas...

This kiss was different, deeper. She felt it all through her body, as if just their lips touching meant he was already a part of her. She leaned back; he stayed with her. She wrapped an arm around his back; her legs spread a little as she tried to make their bodies fit.

They wouldn't *fit* until all these clothes were out of the way...

She pulled her mouth from his. "I don't suppose you have..."

"I don't, not with me. Are you on..."

"No. It hasn't been... necessary." Not for a very long time.

"I want you more than I've ever wanted anything, and I don't think I'll make it until tonight. Wait right here while I run home and grab what I need."

Olive responded by leaning up and in, kissing him too quickly, and then jumping off the couch. Who needed a sexy red dress? "Go."

"I'll be right back." Tuck stood and headed toward the door. Before he got there, his phone rang. He checked the caller ID, then answered with a short, sharp, "What?" He listened a moment, then looked back at her. His face fell.

Before he said a word, she knew he was *not* going to be right back with a condom or condoms.

He stuffed the phone back in his pocket. "Emergency at The Magnolia. I have to go."

"Will I still see you at six?"

At least he was honest. "I don't know. I'll call you."

Talk about deflated. "Be careful," she said as he left, leaving her alone. She normally loved being alone...

Olive sighed as the door closed behind Tuck. It was all she could do to not chase after him. If she did, if she opened that door and called his name, that would be all she wrote. It wasn't like this was going to take long! But she wasn't on any kind of birth control, and he didn't have a handy condom. They weren't kids with zero self-control, and neither of them was stupid enough to think they'd be okay *just this one time*. "There's a fine line between brave and foolish, isn't there?" she muttered. "When have I ever been *brave*?"

She decided to be optimistic about whatever emergency had called Tuck away. He'd get things taken care of. She'd don her sexy red dress and heels, they'd have dinner — maybe — then he'd help her out of that sexy outfit. She grabbed the coffee cups, one empty and one almost empty, and placed them in the sink to wash later.

When the knock sounded on the door, she jumped. *Tuck*, had to be. Maybe the emergency was over, he'd collected what he needed, and... Who else would knock on her door?

He'd just been gone a few minutes; she hadn't locked the door, not yet. The knob turned; the door swung open. Her heart almost came through her throat.

And then...

"Mike!" she said, hoping she didn't sound too disappointed. "Girls!"

Her nieces ran into the room. They never walked anywhere.

Their preferred method of movement seemed to be tied between running and jumping. They entered her little rental house utilizing both.

"Sorry," Mike said. "Dawn said you'd probably be here by now, and the kids really wanted to see you." He lowered his voice as he neared her. "My folks loaded them up with sugar after lunch and we're paying the price. They were making Dawn crazy, which to be honest isn't all that hard these days."

Four-year-old Ava ran to the back corner of the living room, stood by a bookcase, and said, "Arrrrr, matey."

Willow, a much more mature seven, explained. "Ava likes to visit her imaginary friend who lives here. He's a pirate."

"Ava has imaginary friends?"

"Tons," Willow said.

Mike chimed in from the place he'd claimed on the couch, where minutes earlier Tuck had been sitting. "It's exhausting."

Thank goodness Tuck had gotten that call! What if Mike and the girls had walked in at an inopportune time? Another note to herself for tonight. Lock the door.

Willow danced to the Christmas tree. "You used to be a ballerina," she said as she struck a dancer's pose. Well, she tried to but that was no pose Olive had ever seen.

"I did," she said.

"Can you teach me? I want to be a ballerina, like you. Mommy said you were very good."

Not good enough to survive the fall... "Maybe one day, when you're a little older, I can show you a few moves."

Willow tried to spin around, but she stumbled and landed on her behind. Oh, that face! She was disgusted by her performance.

"When you fall, you get up and try again," Olive said. Her heart seemed to skip a beat. That was good advice. Too bad she hadn't taken it herself. That was enough about dancing! "A pirate, huh?" she asked as she turned toward her youngest niece.

Ava joined them. "Yes! It's so hard to tell what he's saying, sometimes. He growls and mumbles and some of his words sound funny."

"*Your* words sound funny," Willow said to her sister.

Ava stuck out her tongue, then turned an angelic face to Olive. "His name is Giles, and he's lived here a very long time. Too long, he says. He likes you better than the last lassie who lived here. She was an old biddy and not as pretty as you and she never kissed anybody like that." Ava looked over her shoulder. "Like what?" There was a brief pause before the child continued. "I think you're confused, Giles." In that moment, little Ava looked an awful lot like her mother. Same bossy tone of voice, too.

"Oh, oh, Giles says you should be brave."

Olive's stomach twisted, and for a moment felt like it was going to jump into her throat. Maybe she'd misheard. Where did that *be brave* come from? Desperate to change the subject, she said, "Who wants cookies?"

Mike groaned. "This is not going to help matters. They've had enough sugar!" The girls jumped on their father and argued, as they squirmed, that they had *not* had too much sugar, proving his point.

With her attention diverted, Ava had stopped talking to her pirate friend. Her *invisible* friend.

Olive stood still as Mike gathered up his girls and told them, in as stern a voice as he could manage, that they couldn't have any more cookies. The girls pouted and begged in a simultaneous whine, and Mike gave in. Just one, he said. They each grabbed one cookie from the box on the coffee table, arguing about which shape they preferred. Bells or wreaths? They'd had their outing, now it was time to head home. She apologized to

Mike for offering sweets before checking with him, but he didn't seem all that concerned. The kids had needed a break, and they'd gotten one.

There were hugs and kisses from the girls, one last check of the Christmas tree, and a wave, from Ava directed toward the bookcase. *Be brave.*

Olive locked the door behind them. All afternoon she'd been obsessed with Tuck and what she wanted to happen, what was *going* to happen. Now a new thought dominated her thoughts.

Did this charming blue house on Jasmine Street come complete with its own pirate ghost?

# CHAPTER 9

Tuck needed a distraction, with everything that was going on in his life. Olive was a great, unexpected, pleasant distraction. Blood on The Magnolia floor and his daytime bartender in tears didn't help matters at all. Whenever he came to work and found the Seawolf Beach Police Chief waiting for him, it was sure to be a bad day.

Ginny, who'd been called in just as he had, was doing her best to calm a hysterical Jodie, who sat on the floor a few feet beyond her usual station. Tuck glanced at the cut on her arm, made a quick judgment, and sent Ginny to his office for the first-aid kit. There was plenty of blood, but as far as he could tell the injury wasn't terrible. He sat on the floor next to Jodie to closely inspect the cut, then asked, in a calm voice, "What happened?"

Mac stood over them, arms crossed, scowl on his face. "Apparently a couple of guys got into a fight..."

Tuck held up one silencing finger. "I want Jodie to tell me what happened."

Mac grumbled, "No one gives me the finger, Tucker."

Tuck shook his finger one more time, because he could. "Do

me a favor and start up the jukebox. B-17." A nice, slow, soothing song would help Jodie relax.

Mac obeyed, but he didn't like it.

Who didn't like "Unchained Melody"?

As soon as the music started, Jodie relaxed. "Unchained Melody" for the win, every time. Ginny returned with the huge first-aid kit Tuck kept in his office, always fully stocked.

"We can call..." Tuck began.

"No," Jodie snapped before he finished. "No ambulance, no trip to the hospital."

"You could use a couple of stitches," he said, keeping his voice calm.

"Butterfly bandages will do just as well," Jodie argued.

She wasn't wrong. "Whatever you want." He opened the kit and went to work. The wound, which didn't look nearly so bad when it was cleaned, was easy enough to bandage. With the blood cleaned off her arm, Jodie closed her eyes and took a deep breath. She listened to the music, got lost in it, let it *ease* her. After a couple of minutes she almost seemed herself again.

"It wasn't any of the regulars. I didn't recognize these guys at all," she said. "When they started in on each other, I figured it was just another minor dustup. The guys usually listen to me when I tell them to cut it out, to calm down. I stepped into the middle of it just as the little one pulled a knife."

"She was lucky," Mac said from his recently claimed seat a couple of tables away. "It didn't take long to find out these are bad dudes. They're locked up, for now. I expect they'll stay where they are for a while."

With the cut bandaged and his daytime bartender considerably calmer, Tuck stood and helped her gently to her feet. "Ginny, why don't you take Jodie home."

The expression on Jodie's face alarmed him. She was truly scared. "I can't go home! What if they know where I live? What if they have friends hanging around? I'm a witness. It wouldn't be hard to find me, everyone knows where I live and I live alone so..."

The offenders were locked up, and even if they weren't it wasn't as if Jodie had been the target. She'd simply gotten in their way. And the witness bit? Every customer who'd been here when it happened could be called a witness. The truth was, Jodie was upset and not thinking clearly. It wouldn't be a good idea for her to be alone tonight.

Tuck looked at Ginny. Did his face fall as much as he thought it did? Didn't matter. He didn't have a choice. "Take the night off. Get your kid, if you want, order a meal for the three of you, on me. Keep an eye on her," he added in a lowered voice.

"What about the bar? You said you were taking the night off?"

He felt his promising evening with Olive melting away. He'd never find a decent fill-in bartender that he trusted, not on a Saturday night. "My plans changed. I'll handle everything." Starting with cleaning the blood off the floor.

When things here settled down a bit he'd call Olive and make his excuses. Maybe she'd forgive him. Maybe not.

When the women were gone, Mac took a stool at the bar. Since he was in uniform he wouldn't drink, but Tuck knew what kind of soda he liked. He grabbed a bottle from the fridge and set it in front of the police chief.

"What was with the jukebox?" Mac asked.

"Music sometimes helps when a person's hurt or stressed. Or both."

"Soothes the savage beast kind of thing?"

"Close enough."

"I hope you didn't have a hot date tonight," Mac said. Was he a freakin' mind reader? Tuck was almost always here on weekend nights. "Looks like you're stuck."

"It's my place," he answered simply.

"I hear you," Mac mumbled as he opened his soda.

Tuck didn't think he needed to be concerned about the safety of his employees, but he was responsible for them all so he had to ask, "Are these guys Jodie's worried about going to be a problem?"

"Nope. They're wanted in half a dozen jurisdictions. I expect they'll be out of town and in another department's hands by Monday. Until then, they're not going anywhere."

"I hope so." Since the place was empty at the moment and Tuck was stranded here... "You're good friends with Colt, aren't you?"

Mac shrugged a little but answered, "Sure."

"This whole thing with him talking to himself all the time, is he okay? Is there something weird going on?"

"Yeah, yeah, the ghosts. I can't talk about it."

"You just did," Tuck grumbled.

"I suppose so." He didn't look at all concerned about his slip of the tongue. "Funny, you'd think finding out something like that, the thing I can't talk about, would be more earth-shattering. But it's really not."

*Not for you, maybe.* "I just wondered..."

Mac guzzled the last of his soda, stood, and headed for the door. "If you have questions, ask Colt."

And he was gone.

Tuck pulled his cell out of his pocket and dialed. He did *not* call Colt.

∽

IT WAS A LITTLE EARLY, but Olive laid out her red dress and high-heeled shoes and jumped in the shower. She wanted her hair to be freshly washed and styled. Makeup was arranged on the counter. She didn't use a lot of cosmetics, but tonight she was going all out. She might even get into the eye shadow, which she almost never used.

As she stepped out of the shower, she heard her cell ringing. Wrapped in a towel, she stepped into the bedroom and snagged the phone. She didn't recognize the number.

"Hello?"

Tuck's voice was unmistakable. She didn't simply hear Tuck, she felt him. "Hi. I got your number from Mike."

"Did you tell him we were going out tonight?" She wasn't sure she wanted her sister to know. At least, not yet.

"No. He was in a rush and didn't question why I needed my neighbor's number."

Typical Mike... "Just as well, I suppose."

"Look, I'm sorry but..."

Olive's heart plummeted. A drop of cool water from her wet hair dribbled down onto her shoulder. *I'm sorry but* was never a good start to a conversation.

"I have to work tonight, and I'll be here super late. Can we reschedule?"

"Sure," she said as casually as possible. The single word tried to stick in her throat.

"Maybe tomorrow night?"

She shook her head, sending more cold droplets onto her shoulder. "Can't. I'm supposed to spend the day with Dawn. We made plans last night, and I really can't..." Can't. Shouldn't. "My Sunday is booked, I'm afraid."

"The whole day?" Tuck sounded horrified.

His tone of voice made her smile. "We're making cookies with the girls, then Mike's mom is cooking a big supper. I've begged off family time twice this week. I don't think I can get away with it again."

He grumbled a bit, then said, "How about Monday night?"

"Monday would be great."

"Six?"

"Make it seven," she said. The boutique didn't close until five, and sometimes customers hung around after closing. She wanted time to get ready. As if she wasn't ready *now*.

Would Tuck find a way to change his plans for tonight if she told him she was naked? Maybe, but if he didn't how humiliated would she be?

"Seven it is," he said. "I'm really sorry."

"Don't be. It's okay." It was *not* okay, but she wouldn't tell him so. "Monday will be perfect." Actually *right now* would be perfect, but...

She heard music in the background. It was too early for a live band, she assumed, and what she heard sounded like a recording. The jukebox, maybe. "Baby It's Cold Outside." She could get dressed, *not* in her red dress, and head to The Magnolia as she had last night. Another burger and *one* can of wine, this time. Maybe Tuck would have time to talk to her in between customers. With luck, there wouldn't be any brawls that sprawled in her direction.

But he didn't invite her, and she didn't want to appear overly eager.

"What will you do tonight?" he asked.

"I don't know. The TV has an antenna that picks up a couple of local stations. I'll find a movie to watch, and I might finish off the cookies."

"I like *Elf*," he said.

She hadn't watched a Christmas movie in years, had actively avoided them. But she remembered the thrill of those movies that were only on TV during December. She and Dawn had spent many a winter break in front of the TV, huddled under their softest blankets. "I prefer *Miracle on 34th Street*. The original, of course."

He grunted a little. "*It's a Wonderful Life.*"

"No." She laughed. "That one always makes me cry."

"We can't have that."

There was a pause, a moment of silence. Neither of them said they had to go, or even a simple goodbye or see you later.

It was Olive who broke the silence. "Maybe I'm over my intense dislike of Christmas. This year is shaping up to be..." *Special. Exciting. Merry.* "...Nice."

"Look, maybe I can..." Before he could finish that sentence, someone in the background shouted his name. That *"Tuck!"* sounded urgent, though how could she know? He finished with, "Shit, I gotta go."

And the call was over.

Olive tossed her phone onto the bed and dropped the towel. She remembered her pirate ghost, or the *possibility* of her ghost, and snatched the towel up to cover herself again. Was he watching? "Get lost, Giles," she whispered.

As she walked toward the dresser to grab pajamas, she found herself humming.

*Baby it's cold outside...*

# CHAPTER 10

A typical Saturday night at The Magnolia combined with thoughts of Olive and a Monday night date kept Tuck's mind off the news Colt had shared earlier in the week. At least, ghosts and grandmothers weren't *all* he thought about as he poured drinks, talked to customers, and kept the peace when it was necessary. He was glad to be busy with other things, happy to have his mind on other matters. He wasn't yet sure what to do with the information Colt had shared, if anything.

In quiet moments his mind wandered, and as the crowd thinned and quieted, unwanted thoughts came roaring back.

Colt had dropped a real bombshell. Tuck could've spent the past couple of days searching family trees on the Internet or hiring a PI to do the search for him, but he'd done neither. Did he really want to know? He hadn't decided. His mother, gone more than twenty years now, would've loved to know her birth mother. She would've cherished the story of Phillip and Maude and latched onto the fact that her parents had loved one another so much.

He wasn't a sentimental person; years ago he'd accepted that he had no living family and wouldn't, unless the day came that he made his own. A wife. Kids. He'd never even come close.

Tuck couldn't afford to get lost in sentimentality, but finding out he'd had a grandmother living right down the street all these years hit him hard. Harder than he'd expected. His carefully constructed world had been turned upside down, and he didn't like it at all.

He could choose to simply ignore what Colt had told him or write the entire story off to fantasy, a crazy man's hallucination. Why not? What difference did it make? He wasn't about to burst in on Maude's family, when and if he identified them, with a big "Surprise!" No one wanted long-lost relatives showing up on their doorstep, especially this time of year. Unless he had some kind of proof, they'd write him off as a con man. Or a crazy person.

To be honest, he felt a little crazy at the moment. Between the granny news and Olive, that wasn't a surprise.

To take his mind off ghosts, he pondered where to take Olive Monday. Two days seemed a very long time to wait. Could he show up at her house in the middle of the night? Tonight? Sure. Would she let him in? Probably. But he didn't want to do it that way. She deserved better. She deserved a real date, a special evening before they went where he was damn sure they were headed.

Unfortunately he'd already taken her to Maggie's, which was the best place for a date in Seawolf Beach. The other options were too noisy, too crowded. The music was too loud. They could drive over to Biloxi, as he'd planned to tonight, but he didn't want to be that far way from home when they were done. It wasn't that far, but still... far enough.

She'd said that this year Christmas was *nice*. He had to admit, he didn't feel as much a Scrooge about the holiday as he normally did. Olive wouldn't be here much longer, but while she was around... was it possible they were actually good for one another? He'd never thought himself a positive influence on anyone. He'd especially never expected to be the one to bolster anyone's Christmas spirit.

Olive was a special woman. She deserved to be treated like one. No man should ever drop her again.

When inspiration hit, he started making phone calls. Those calls took his mind off surprise relatives, lost grannies, and everything else. Everything else but Olive.

∼

OLIVE DIDN'T BAKE, so the process with Dawn and her kiddies was challenging. The rest of the year there was no reason for her to spend an entire day in the kitchen. Why make cookies or cake for one? There was a great bakery close to her condo where she could buy a couple of cookies, or a slice of cake, or a small loaf of freshly baked bread. It wasn't like she had anyone to bake for at home.

Baking with children was messy. Fun, filled with laughter, but messy and chaotic. Dawn's lovely, large kitchen was in turmoil, likely not for the first time. Dawn didn't seem to mind the noise, the flour all over the floor, or the screeching. Oh, the screeching.

A few hours after the process began, they had several containers of freshly baked cookies placed throughout the kitchen. Chocolate chip. Gingerbread. Oatmeal raisin. The misshapen cookies were set to the side for the bakers — and Mike — to test, while the prettier ones were saved for friends. One big box went into the freezer, the only way to save them for Dawn and Mike's annual Christmas Eve gathering. The baby was due Christmas Eve. What was Dawn thinking, to keep that tradition! The baby could come early, or late, which could change their plans in a heartbeat. Who knew with babies?

Not her.

When Olive had asked her sister why she didn't just schedule a C-section, Dawn had become almost angry, for a moment. If it was necessary, sure, she'd do it, but her daughters had come into the world in a natural way and her son would do the same. Giving birth wasn't supposed to be convenient.

Olive wasn't sure she agreed, but arguing with Dawn these days wasn't wise.

Willow and Ava were adorable, loving, energetic girls. But they were also a full-time job. Now a little boy would be thrown into the mix. How would Dawn manage? Three kids, a husband, a household, a business...

Olive turned away to look out the back window for a long moment. Was that gnawing sensation in her gut *envy*?

Nope. No way. If she did feel a bit of jealousy, it was some weird biological thing. A ticking clock Tuck had wound up tight and left unsprung.

She wondered if he was awake yet. He worked late. What time would he get up on a Sunday?

Nope. No. She was too old and too careful to chase after any man.

Ava danced her way to Olive, who'd just taken a seat at the kitchen table with a misshapen chocolate chip cookie in hand. Dawn had been sitting for a while, with her own cookie. A gingerbread man with no head.

"Rosaline is very sad that she can't have a cookie," Ava said as she twirled. "She misses cookies. Among other things, but she won't tell me what the other things are. She says I'm too young to hear about it. I'm not too young. I'm four years old!"

A ghost or an active imagination? What about Giles? The whole thing about a pirate ghost seeing her and Tuck kissing, that was impossible, right? *Be brave.* The kiss had been... a lucky guess. Had to be. As for the *be brave*, she must've misheard. Ava didn't always speak clearly. Maybe she'd been trying to say something else, a completely ordinary word Olive had no hope of deciphering.

Yeah, right.

There was no reason to alarm Dawn with these questions, but... "How many invisible friends does Ava have?"

Dawn sighed. "Three, but Rosaline seems to be the most popular. I know she'll outgrow this one day, but for now it's exhausting."

Mike had said the same thing. *Exhausting.* That state was a constant with children, or so it seemed.

"I can imagine." Olive's logical mind wouldn't allow her to believe that ghosts were real and her niece saw them, but she had to push past her own logic and accept that maybe she didn't know all. It was more than Ava and her invisible friends that had her questioning. Adding Colt to the mix complicated everything. Who was she to say what was possible and what was not?

"You haven't said much about running the store," Dawn said.

"I've said plenty." She tried not to complain, but she did keep her sister up-to-date on sales and inventory.

"It's challenging, I know, or can be. Some days more than others."

Olive leaned into the table to be closer to her sister. "How do you do it? Day after day. I mean, most of the customers are lovely, they really are, but it seems like every day there's *one*. The bad apple that spoils the bunch."

"I've learned to take them in stride."

"Maybe in the next week and a half I'll learn to do the same, but I suspect it might take longer." Not quite a week and a half. Nine days.

Dawn laughed at her, and Olive smiled in response, but her

stomach knotted. She didn't let her response show. Nine days, Christmas Day, and then a day or two later she'd head home. Leaving her sister, this amazing family that should include a new baby at that point, and Tuck behind.

Nine days...

~

THIS YEAR IS SHAPING *up to be...*

She'd finished, after a pause, with *nice*. But was that where she'd been going? How else might Olive have finished that sentence? This year is shaping up to be better. Extraordinary. Life-changing.

Special would do.

He should've gotten up early. There was so much to do. Instead he'd slept in, staying in bed long after Olive would've headed for work, dreaming of their upcoming date. No one would interrupt them tonight. There would be no change of plans, no emergency at The Magnolia. If there was, he'd just tell whoever was in charge to call Mac, kick everyone out, and lock the doors.

Colt tried to call a couple of times. He texted. The man would not give up! Tuck didn't answer. He didn't even read the texts. One day he was going to have to deal with what he'd been told, but not today. Not tomorrow, either. Next year, after the holidays were over... he'd think about it.

Olive made him forget everything. She was a much-needed escape from reality. Could he call a ghost granny *reality*?

He'd bought his house on Jasmine Street on a whim. The Magnolia did good business, especially in tourist season. He had to spend his money on something, unlike Uncle Houston who'd squirreled away his profits — which had also been left to his only living relative, Tuck — and lived simply. This was a great house but was definitely too big for one man. It wasn't like he had real prospects for more or dreamed of having a family to fill the empty rooms. Sure, the vague possibility had occurred to him a time or two, but that possibility seemed as likely as the chance of being bitten by an insect and turning into a superhero.

Neither was likely to happen. He managed to run off every woman who expressed anything other than interest in a one — or two — night stand.

He'd always thought the idea of the perfect family was a lie. The house was just for him, even if he didn't use much more than a quarter of it. His bedroom upstairs; the kitchen; the sunroom; the den, with a comfortable recliner and big TV. He didn't entertain, so the other rooms got dusty and stale.

Why did that seem kinda sad to him today?

His doorbell rang right at one. Tuck was waiting, so he answered the door quickly. Jodie looked better than she had Saturday night, but her arm was still bandaged. Ginny was, well, the same as always. Tough expression. Shoulders squared. Eyes alert.

Everything they needed for today's job had been delivered an hour ago. "Thanks, guys," he said as he let them inside. They'd never been to his home, so they looked around with open curiosity. He didn't question that they seemed surprised by his living quarters. "Everything you'll need is here." He gestured to the boxes and bags sitting on the floor.

Ginny crossed her arms. "Why aren't you doing this yourself?"

*I don't know how. I don't do Christmas. I need help...*

"I figured y'all could use the extra money."

"Overtime pay, right?" Jodie asked.

"Yes. And a nice Christmas bonus."

Ginny looked at Jodie and smiled. "Fine. Let's get to work."

# CHAPTER 11

The day should've gone by quickly, but it didn't. The minutes seemed to drag. Dawn's Radiance stayed busy with shoppers looking for Christmas presents or special outfits for parties and family gatherings. Olive did her best to help them all, but her mind wandered.

Boy, did it wander. Tonight was going to be epic. Wasn't it?

Until today, Olive had never left Dawn's Radiance for lunch or any other reason. The Christmas crowd kept her busy enough, and she didn't want to miss a sale. For Dawn's sake. Kids were expensive, and Dawn was about to have three of them.

She hung a sign on the door and locked it behind her. Lunch was not on her mind.

Normally she'd duck and cover, put her head down and explain away everything that had happened to her since coming to Seawolf Beach. Tuck. Ava and her invisible friends. A freakin' ghost in her house! *Tuck.*

*Brave* wasn't a term anyone would choose to describe her, but she could try. Would Tuck think the dress she'd bought for tonight was sexy? That's what he'd asked for, *sexy*. Sexy wasn't Olive's style, never had been. When she'd been on stage she wanted people looking at her, but off the stage? In real life? She was happy to melt into the background and let someone else stand out. Her new outfit was definitely a step up. Was it brave or foolish?

There were a couple of blocks between Dawn's Radiance and Hart's Vinyl Depot, an easy walk on a mild December day. Olive had never been inside the depot. Not only had she not had time to shop since arriving in Seawolf Beach, she didn't own a record player.

Thank goodness there was a coffee bar. She could use that as an excuse for her stop.

Anna manned the coffee bar. Did she know her guy saw ghosts? How could she not?

"Small coffee, please," Olive said as she approached the counter. "Cream and sugar." While Anna made the coffee, Olive turned and looked around the place. The public area was massive, with rows of bins in the center, boxes of sale records against one wall, the coffee bar, and a little bit of seating. The bench near the front window looked ancient but solid. There were a couple of employees, several customers browsing, but no Colt.

Maybe that was just as well. How did one ask if the place they'd rented was haunted?

"How are you liking the house? Everything okay?" Anna asked.

"It's great. I love it." Olive placed cash on the counter, started to take a sip and decided the coffee was still too hot, and backed up a step. Again, she looked around the depot. "I don't see Colt. Is he here?"

"He's in the back, cleaning some old records that just came in. Is there a problem? If there is, I can handle it for you."

Was a pirate ghost a problem she could share with Anna? Maybe this wasn't such a great idea, coming here with a half-baked plan. "No, like I said, I love the house. It's great." She could, probably should, offer Anna a polite goodbye, then turn around and walk out, coffee in hand. No one had to know that she'd come in here with impossible questions dancing through her brain. *Brave.*

"My neighbor Tuck has become kind of a friend since I came here." She hated that her voice shuddered when she said *friend,* but she ignored the telling tremble and barreled forward.

"I know," Anna said. She smiled, a little. "A friend or more than a friend?"

"Just a friend." *For now.* "We were talking." There was that shudder again.

The expression on Anna's face changed subtly. Her smile faded as she whispered, "Did he tell you?"

Olive didn't play coy and ask *what.* The look on her face probably told it all.

"He did, didn't he?" Anna rounded the counter. When she was close to Olive, she whispered, "Tuck was shaken, and I get it, I do. That kind of news is bound to be upsetting. If Colt was up front about what he can do, what he sees, maybe people wouldn't be so shocked when he knows things he shouldn't. He really doesn't want everyone to know. I don't know why, but I do my best to respect his wishes. If it was me I'd tell everyone. I mean, it's pretty amazing, right?"

*She knew.* Anna knew *everything.*

Olive could understand why Colt would want to keep his ability a secret. She would, if she was in his shoes. "I don't know what this has to do with Tuck, but..."

Anna backed up a step. "I thought you said he told you."

"He asked if I believe in ghosts, and we started talking, and..."

"You're not here about Tuck's grandmother."

*Grandmother?* "No, I'm sorry." Was that why he'd been so

upset when she'd gone to deliver the scarves? Some kind of unwanted news from his dead grandmother?

"Colt is going to kill me," Anna said under her breath.

"I don't plan to tell anyone anything, but I... I have a couple of questions." More now that Tuck had become a part of the conversation.

"I can imagine."

First things first. "Is there a pirate ghost living in my house?"

Anna's back straightened. "You saw..."

"Not me. My niece, Ava."

"Come on." Anna indicated with a wave of her hand that Olive was to join her.

What she really wanted to do was finish her coffee, get back to work, then maybe ask if it was too late to stay with Dawn and her family. What difference would that make? Ava had other "invisible friends," like Rosaline. Were they everywhere? Olive stayed rooted to the spot. What had she been thinking to come here? Why ask questions she didn't really want answered?

When Anna was halfway across the room, she turned and motioned again, since Olive hadn't moved. "Since I spilled the beans, might as well make the best of it. Colt could use your help."

Reluctantly, Olive headed in Anna's direction. She stopped to take a sip of coffee. For courage? Maybe. She walked slowly, uncertainly. When she reached Anna she asked in a lowered voice, "How can I possibly help?"

Together they walked toward the back of the depot. "I'm not sure, but Maude is driving Colt nuts. Until this thing with Tuck is resolved she won't move on and she won't give Colt a moment's peace."

Maude must be Tuck's grandmother. This was more than Olive had bargained for, more than she was willing to take on. Sleeping with Tuck was one thing. Running interference between him, a man who saw ghosts, and a dead grandmother was a different story.

The back room was bigger than she'd expected, dimmer, not as colorful as the public space. It really did look like a place ghosts would haunt, if they could. If they did. As they approached a small room near the back, they heard Colt talking. She couldn't make out the words, but he was definitely talking to someone. Living or dead? When they could see through the open doorway, it appeared Colt was alone. So, *dead*. If not for Ava and her pirate friend, Olive would think he was off his rocker.

Anna called out, a simple, "Hey," which was both a greeting and a warning to let him know he was no longer alone. The conversation stopped.

"Sorry, I was just talking to myself," he said.

Anna walked into the small room, gave Colt a quick kiss, and then said, "She knows."

He didn't look happy to hear that news.

"Her niece saw the pirate in the Jasmine Street house. Also, she and Tuck are friends or dating or something and the subject of ghosts came up. I'm afraid I told her about Maude before I found out she didn't already know. Sorry."

*We're not actually dating*, Olive started to say, but... in a way they were. *Or something* was more accurate. Even if dinner a couple of days ago hadn't been an actual date, tonight's dinner would be. What was she to Tuck? What was he to her?

"How old is your niece?" Colt asked.

"Four."

Colt nodded, then tossed aside the microfiber towel he'd been using. "If she holds to form, she'll stop seeing them in a year or so."

"*Them* being ghosts," Olive clarified.

"Yes."

She had a million questions; she didn't know where to start. So she took another sip of coffee while she tried to decide what to ask first.

"I'm glad you're here," Colt said after a pause of his own. "Maude thinks you can help."

She'd come here to ask about Giles, but she'd stumbled into something entirely new, and complicated. Would it be cowardly to turn and run?

It would. "I don't know what I can possibly do, but... I'm listening."

∼

OLIVE WALKED HOME BRISKLY, with a spring in her step in spite of everything Colt had told her. She didn't want to think about it, didn't believe there was any way she could help. Best, for now, to focus on the evening ahead.

She'd have plenty of time to get ready, since she'd told Tuck to pick her up at seven instead of his suggested six. Six would've been better. She could've rushed! Now she'd be ready early and she'd sit, twiddling her thumbs, waiting for him to arrive. A shower, some makeup, a bit of time on her hair and then she could slip into the new red dress and those shoes.

She didn't want to think about ghosts, not Giles and not Maude. For a few hours maybe she could make herself focus only on the living.

As she approached her house she couldn't help but notice the changes to Tuck's place. When she'd first arrived at her rental, she'd appreciated that he hadn't decorated for the holiday. While she'd been at work today, that had changed. There was a wreath on the front door. A Christmas tree in the window, colorful lights sparkling. There was even greenery on the porch banister.

"Traitor," she whispered as she walked by, but then she smiled a little. Maybe going overboard for Christmas wasn't such a bad thing, after all. She was beginning to enjoy the lights, at least.

She couldn't run from *The Nutcracker* incident forever. No one could hide from the holidays year after year after year, though she'd tried. The memory of that night and what she'd lost in one bad instant had gone on too long. The fall, the *drop*, had robbed her of so much.

Tuck's truck wasn't in the driveway, so it was safe to assume he wasn't in his house, watching her. She stopped on the sidewalk and turned to admire the decorations for a moment. That was all the time she had. A moment. Getting ready for tonight was going to take some time, even if she was overly anxious and questioning her suggested delay in the date start time.

Thinking about Tuck was enough to make her forget, for a moment, that there was a ghost in her house.

Ghosts! Everywhere, apparently. She thought again about Colt's request. Did she want to help? Tuck wouldn't listen to her just because they were testing the boundaries, trying to figure out what they were, if they were anything at all. And the other thing... talk about stepping out of her comfort zone! Why couldn't Anna handle it? Or Colt himself? She'd left the depot this afternoon with a noncommittal, *I'll think about it*. What else could she say?

All she needed to think about right now was tonight. Would the night go where she expected it to? Of course it would. What could stop them?

Nothing that she could think of.

She unlocked her front door, walked inside, and dropped her bags on the couch. Next the lights on her own tree were switched on. Maybe she'd turned her back on all things

Christmas for a few years, but the lights were pretty. Why should she deny herself that small enjoyment?

As she walked toward the bathroom with a shower in mind, she called out in a voice that, surprisingly, revealed no trepidation. "No peeking, Giles!"

~

TUCK KNOCKED on Olive's door precisely at seven o'clock. Given everything that had happened lately he shouldn't be so damn happy, but he was. Olive helped him forget it all for a while, just by being.

He was never at a loss for words, but when she opened the door he couldn't speak. She was always beautiful. In sweatpants and a ridiculously oversized T-shirt she was gorgeous. But now, in this moment...

"Wow." *Lady in red...* The dress wasn't super short or super tight, but it showed off Olive's impressive curves and killer legs. Maybe she didn't dance anymore, but she still had a dancer's legs. How could a woman look so damn sexy with that shy, uncertain expression on her face? Olive wasn't bold; the dress was.

She stepped outside and turned to lock the door behind her. The rear view was just as impressive as the front. They might not make it to dinner...

He offered his arm, and she took it as she walked gingerly down the steps in those high heels that made her legs look even more fantastic. Before the night was over, he'd have those dancer's legs wrapped around him.

"So, where are we going?" she asked as they hit the sidewalk.

"Not far. We can walk."

Her headed jerked up; she glared at him. "Walk? In these heels?"

"Trust me." When they turned from the sidewalk onto the walkway to his front porch, she relaxed. "I decided I didn't want to share you tonight."

She might've been insulted, but she wasn't. At least, she didn't appear to be, and he thought he had a pretty good read on her. "So this dress and these heels are just for you?"

"They are. Do you mind?"

"Not at all." She stopped at the bottom of the steps. "You decorated your house for Christmas." It was a simple statement with no element of shock or judgment. She would've seen the new decorations on her way home, so there was no need for surprise.

"Seemed like a good idea at the time."

She continued to study the changes he'd made. Well, changes Ginny and Jodie had made on his behalf. "You know, the first thing I really liked about you was that your house *wasn't* decorated."

"I'll tear it all down right now."

She laughed. "No, I like it. It seems right. Maybe this trip is helping me to shed my curmudgeon-like attitude toward Christmas. It's silly, really, that I've let one bad holiday ruin every December for years." They climbed the steps, and she asked, "Did you cook?"

"Oh no. I wanted you to enjoy the evening, not run screaming back to your house for another omelet."

"I like omelets."

What did it take to rattle her? More than a bar brawl, more than having her December turned upside down to help her sister, more than a whirlwind romance with a brand-new neighbor. Did Olive ever get rattled?

He opened the front door to a small entryway. Beyond was the living room, which now boasted a tall, lavishly decorated and brightly lit tree. No tasteful white lights for him, no, he wanted every color in the rainbow on his Christmas tree. Olive might think it was tacky.

She released his arm and walked over to the tree to study it more closely. She looked up, down, around, even checked out the backside that faced the front window, then declared, "It's beautiful."

Olive in red, standing by the first Christmas tree he'd ever owned as an adult, that was true beauty.

"Dinner is getting cold," he said. Olive left the tree behind to rejoin him. She took his arm again and they walked down the hallway, through the kitchen, then onto the large screened porch that looked out over his wooded backyard.

"Wow, this is surprising. Gorgeous, but I wouldn't expect a volunteer fireman to leave this many candles burning."

"There's a fire blanket on standby and a small fire extinguisher in that corner." He pointed. "It wouldn't have the same effect if I had to come out here and light all the candles while you waited in the kitchen. You'd get bored, and hungry."

Olive looked up at him with those deep brown eyes, her lush lips slightly parted, her breath short. "Nate Tucker, you are many things, but in my experience you are never boring."

∾

THE SCENE before her was like something out of a movie or a dream. A small round table was set with china, crystal, and silver. A warming tray sat in the middle, and prepared salads had been placed to the side. A bottle of wine — no cans for them tonight — was on ice. Candles burned there, on other tables scattered about, even on the floor. It was the most romantic fire hazard she'd ever seen.

"I've never seen anything quite like this," she said. "Not in real life. In the movies, maybe, but... Did you do all this?"

"I can't take credit. I picked up dinner from Maggie's. They even provided the dishes and silverware. I'm more of a paper plate kind of guy."

"Shrimp and grits?" she asked, her eye on the covered silver tray.

"You seemed to like that the other day, so it seemed a safe choice."

"It was."

She knew where this night was heading, wanted it, needed it even. But before she sat down at this lovely table with a man she was becoming more and more attached to, she had to tell him what was going on. He'd had enough surprises in his life lately. She wouldn't add to the stress he was under. She wouldn't lie to him.

"We need to talk," she said.

"Oh shit," he muttered. "What's wrong?"

"Nothing, really," she said quickly. "I just don't want any secrets between us, not tonight." *Not ever.*

His expression changed; he looked like he expected the worst.

"I went to the depot today, to talk to Colt."

"About me?" he asked.

"Not really. At least, that wasn't the reason I went to the depot. I wanted to know if ghosts were real, and to ask him if there was a pirate ghost in my house. There is, by the way. Ava saw him Saturday. She said his name is Giles."

"You can always stay here if you're afraid of Giles," he said in his usual lighthearted tone of voice, though she detected a hint of new stress.

Olive managed a small smile. She wasn't anywhere near done. "While I was there, Colt asked me to... help."

"With my supposed grandmother? I guess that's where this is headed, right?"

"Yes. I don't believe he would've mentioned it, he didn't intend to break a confidence, but for some reason Anna thought you'd told me and that's why I was there, and she said... too much." This was getting so far out of her comfort zone... "Colt really wants you to call him, to talk this over. Sounds like the ghost is hounding him night and day."

"Not my problem."

She kept going. They needed to get past this so they could move on. Move forward. "Maude is insisting that Colt retrieve the pearl earrings she believes were taken by a woman at the retirement home."

"What does that have to do with me?" Tuck snapped.

She should've waited until after. Until tomorrow. Until... No. Now or never. "Your grandfather gave them to her, and she wants you to have them. She said one day you could give them to... someone you care about." She hesitated to tell Tuck word for word what she'd been told. *One day he can give them to a woman he loves as much as Phillip loved Maude.*

Yeah, she should've waited to tell him about the request. This was ruining the mood. But waiting, telling him after the fact, would've been wrong.

"I don't want the old woman's damn earrings," he said with finality.

"That's fine. I just... I don't want us to start whatever this is with a lie, even a lie of omission, between us."

The tension in his shoulders eased; his eyes softened as he relaxed. "I know very well what this is."

"Me, too," she whispered.

"And... thank you for telling me. Maybe I don't want to hear about it, but you were honest. There aren't enough honest people in the world."

Olive dropped her small handbag onto a chair at the nicely laid table. The evening purse was sparkly and looked great with her dress, but was barely big enough to hold her cell phone and the key to the front door. She should've left the cell at home; there was nothing that couldn't wait. With both hands free she walked to Tuck, stood before him, and took his face in her hands. It was a good face. More than handsome — though his face was quite handsome — it was pleasant, expressive, and becoming so familiar the mere sight touched her.

She kissed him. She'd been craving a kiss all day, had thought about it while she worked, while she showered, while she dressed up. For him. The kiss was like taking a sip of cool water when she was parched. Like sitting down after a long day on her feet. More than a relief, it was pure pleasure.

He kissed her as if he felt the same way. Forget ghosts, retail, any person that wasn't in this room right now. That's what she did as she fell into him. *Forget everything but this.*

"I'm not all that hungry," she said as she pulled away. "Do you have a microwave?"

"Oh, I do," Tuck said. He pulled her in and kissed her again, deeper, more passionately. He pulled away reluctantly, then set to blowing out all the candles. The fireman in him couldn't leave them burning, she supposed. In order to speed things along, she helped. In a couple of minutes the screened-in porch was dark, lit only by light streaming in through the kitchen door and one window.

Tuck took her hand. "Tonight I'm prepared," he said as he led her through the kitchen, down another hallway, and up the stairs to the master bedroom. For a second she wondered if his room was always this neat. Bed made. No dust to be seen. No socks on the floor. Like any of that would've made a difference.

"Good." She was prepared herself, mentally and physically. How could she not be when she'd been thinking about this all day?

He kissed her again, as they stood beside the bed. His hands skimmed her body, learning her curves, arousing her with that touch until everything but this, everything but *him*, faded away.

She ended the kiss, spun around, and lifted her hair. "Unzip me." She'd managed getting the zipper up on her own, but it hadn't been easy.

The zipper was lowered slowly. His fingers brushed her back, down and down and down. When she shrugged off the dress she'd stand before Tuck in nothing but the super sexy black underwear she'd bought just for this occasion.

It *was* an occasion, but she hesitated before shrugging off the dress.

"Damn, Olive Carson. I never saw you coming."

"I didn't expect you, either."

He unbuttoned his shirt, slipped it off, and tossed it onto the floor. She rotated one shoulder, in preparation. In a second, maybe two, the red dress would be on the floor.

In the distance, she heard her cell ring, the sound faint, muted. Tuck heard it, too. His head swiveled toward the door.

"They can leave a message," Olive said. Worst case Dawn might've gone into labor a little bit early. If that had happened Mike would take her to the hospital, his parents would watch the girls, and she'd join them later. They didn't need her, not for this.

Olive kicked off her heels and Tuck toed off his boots. In a couple of minutes, maybe less, they'd both be naked. She wanted that, she did, but she also wanted to savor every second. The night could be over too quickly if she wasn't careful.

It was in her nature to be careful, but maybe she didn't have to be tonight. She couldn't put Tuck and caution in the same sentence. He was wild where she was not. But again, not tonight. She reached out and slipped her hands into the waistband of his unzipped jeans.

His phone, which was still in his back pocket, started to ring.

First her phone and now his. This couldn't be good.

He snagged the phone and answered with a sharp, frustrated, "What!"

The muted, frantic voice she heard on the other end of the call sounded like Mike. Olive couldn't make out many actual words, but she watched as Tuck's expression changed. She made out one word very clearly.

"Help."

# CHAPTER 12

It wasn't much more than a mile to the Woodward house. Normally he'd walk. This was not a night for walking.

"Why can't they just go to the hospital?" Olive asked as she climbed into the passenger seat of his truck.

In a perfect world...

"Mike says there's no time. This third baby is coming fast."

They backed into the street with more speed than normal. Olive bounced in her seat as she screeched, "What are *you* supposed to do about it?"

"Remember I told you I was a bouncer in the Keys?"

"Yes, but..."

"One night a woman in labor came into the bar, looking for her husband who was ignoring her calls. She should've called a cab and gone to the hospital, but she was so mad she didn't."

"You delivered her baby."

"Right there on the bar. I tried to keep her calm, which didn't work by the way, and I stayed calm because I thought the paramedics would get there on time. They were a couple minutes too late, so I delivered the kid."

His passenger responded with a short burst of laughter. Then again, it might've been a stifled scream.

When he got to the Woodward house, he'd assess. Mike said there was no time to get Dawn to the hospital, which in his defense wasn't exactly close. Maybe an ambulance would arrive on time this time around. There might be a paramedic on board who had the proper experience. He could hope. And pray. He never should've told anyone he'd delivered a baby in a bar, but it did make for a good story over a couple of beers.

By the time they pulled up to the curb in front of Mike's house, Olive had pulled herself together. Her spine was stiff, her shoulders squared. It was like she'd purposely shaken off her initial panic and was gearing up for battle.

He should do the same.

The Woodward house was two-story, with a small front yard, a big backyard, and a wide front porch. Mike opened the front door as Tuck and Olive ran up the steps.

"Where is she?" Tuck asked.

"Our bedroom, upstairs at the end of the hall."

He ran in that direction. Olive stayed right behind him. Mike called up the stairs, "I called an ambulance! They said they'd get here as quickly as they could!"

Maybe it would be soon enough. This time.

The upstairs hallway was crowded. Both girls were there, along with Mike's dad, Will. At least Will was leaning up against a wall, not planted in the middle of the narrow hall. The kids ran, laughed, occasionally shouted.

He opened the bedroom door just as Dawn let out a blood-curdling scream. Mike's mom, Susie, who stood at the side of the bed, closed her eyes and tensed for the duration of the scream. She'd been crying.

Tuck kinda wanted to cry himself.

Olive went into action. "Susie, take the girls to the kitchen and make them a snack. Take Will with you." Her tone left no room for argument; everyone obeyed without question.

The scream ended; a red-faced, sweating Dawn panted as she looked up at her sister. "What are you doing here? Get out! Where's Mike?" She looked toward the door, then back at her sister. "Wait a minute. Why are you wearing that dress? And why are you with Tuck! Mike said you didn't answer your phone. Did you forget that you have a pregnant sister?"

That last question was delivered at a decibel that had to be damaging to one's eardrums.

Olive remained calm. "I'm an event planner and this is an event. I'm wearing the dress because I was on a date, believe it or not. Yes, it's been a while, we can discuss later. I didn't answer my phone because it was in another room, and I was... otherwise occupied."

Tuck lifted the sheet. Well, crap, this baby was coming now. *Right now.*

"Dawn, you need to push."

"I'm not ready!"

"Baby number three is. Let's go."

~

THE BABY WAS DELIVERED into the world with no issues, and as soon as that was done, the ambulance arrived. Ten minutes earlier and someone else would've handled the delivery. Tuck had stayed calm, talking in a soothing voice and making sure that the baby was born without any trouble, while Olive stood at the head of the bed and held Dawn's hand. She was pretty sure at least two fingers were broken. Dawn had quite a grip when she was giving birth.

Paramedics moved Dawn to a stretcher and put the newborn, wrapped in blankets, in her arms.

Mike and Susie were going to drive to the hospital to be with the new mother and baby. Will would stay with the girls, who were already in their pajamas. They wouldn't sleep for a while, Olive suspected. They were too wound up.

So was Rosaline, according to Ava.

Olive's heart pounded too hard and probably would for a while, but her part here was done. It was over. Or so she thought. Mike called out to her as she walked down the stairs.

"Dawn wants to talk to you before she goes."

"I'm sure it can wait until tomorrow."

"I tried telling her that. She insists." Oh, the expression on Mike's face! Dawn must've been *very* insistent. First she tells her little sister to get out; now she insists on delaying the trip to the hospital because she wants to *talk*?

Olive walked quickly to the ambulance. A paramedic, who apparently expected her, assisted her into the back where Dawn and the baby waited on the stretcher. They were both in good shape, so maybe there was no rush. Still, everyone would feel better when they were checked out by an actual doctor.

"What do you need?" Olive asked.

Dawn was worn out, tired to the bone, but the look on her face was one of dogged determination. "You can't date Tuck."

"Why not?" Did her sister know something about Tuck that she didn't? Was this a warning?

Why did her mind always go there? She was so skittish, after being burned by a man she'd thought she loved.

Dawn lowered her voice. "He's seen my vagina. You have to end it now!"

Olive smiled; she relaxed as if she were uncoiling from the center of her being outward. She took a moment to study the new baby closely. He was so small and fragile, so amazingly perfect.

"I should be the one who's upset. Tuck saw your lady parts before he saw mine."

"Olive Marie!" Dawn snapped. She sighed and added, "I'm serious."

*So am I...*

A paramedic ordered Olive out; it was time to go.

"We'll talk tomorrow," she said. "Love you, sis."

"Tomorrow will be too late!" Dawn snapped.

As she left the back of the ambulance, Olive muttered, "I certainly hope so."

∽

THE DRIVE HOME WAS QUIET. His truck moved down the residential streets much more slowly than it had on the way to Mike's house.

He half expected Olive to bolt as soon as he turned into the driveway, but she didn't. She left the passenger seat on her own and walked to his porch, not hers.

She'd left her purse inside. That was the reason.

"Not exactly the night I'd planned," he said as he opened the front door, which he hadn't even bothered to lock as they'd left.

Olive laughed lightly. "I imagine not. You must be exhausted. Do you want me to go?"

"I want you to stay."

"I want that, too."

He locked the door behind her. "What did Dawn want when she called you to the ambulance?"

She sighed, hesitated, then answered, "Sister stuff."

He envied Olive her family. She didn't have a husband, no kids of her own, but she had parents, a sister, nieces, and now a nephew. There might be aunts and cousins out there, family reunions, squabbles that didn't last, shared traits they could see in others and in themselves. She had *sister stuff*.

Until he married and had kids of his own — if that ever happened — he wouldn't be a part of any of that. He wanted it, some days he craved it, but the idea also terrified him.

Which was why he was reluctant to look into this crazy Maude story. Was she really his grandmother? He didn't want to think about that now, couldn't let his mind go there.

"I need a shower," he said.

"So do I," Olive whispered.

He took her hand and led her up the stairs.

# CHAPTER 13

She'd never showered with a man before. Stefan had liked his privacy when he bathed, and there hadn't been a man since. So here she was. Another first for her. Tuck's walk-in shower was a good size; they weren't crowded. That didn't mean they moved away from one another. No, they touched constantly. They kissed under the spray of warm water. Tuck washed her back, and then her thighs, and then more.

She'd never expected to be here, with him, but all she could do was live in the moment. She didn't do enough of that. *Live in the moment*. Enjoy the curveballs life threw her way. This trip to Seawolf Beach had been filled with curveballs.

When they were more than clean, Tuck dried her body with a fat gray towel, and she did the same for him. They took their time; they had all night. With every touch, with every second that passed, Olive spiraled closer to losing control. She'd never wanted any man, never wanted *anything*, the way she wanted him. She'd be happy for their first time to be on the floor, or standing in the shower, but they hadn't been thinking ahead. The condoms were on the bedside table, just a few feet away. They wouldn't do any good at all from that distance.

Tuck held onto her as he danced her into the bedroom and grabbed one as they fell onto the bed. She laughed a little as they bounced, but there was no laughter as he kissed one nipple and then the other, as he touched her where she needed him to touch.

Another new sensation; another curveball. She'd never been so ready for a man that she completely lost control. She'd never been this *ready* for anything in her life! She wrapped her legs around him and he was there, inside her, filling her. Relief and a desire for more washed through her; she was caught up in a sensation of connection, *togetherness*, that went beyond the physical. There was nothing in the world but this, nothing but the two of them and the way they fit together.

She could stay here all night, joined with Tuck, letting physical joy wash over her, wanting to wallow in it but also driving toward the end. Control? She had none, wanted none.

She shattered, and he came with her. It had been a long time for her, but she couldn't remember a sensation this powerful, couldn't remember ever being with a man and feeling so... complete.

Could one night with a man change her life? Change *her*? It felt that way.

Tuck lifted his head and smiled at her. "Damn," he whispered.

She wanted to believe that he felt something like she did, in this moment. That this was more, or could be. That this was special. That *they* were special.

Fanciful thoughts.

"Damn, indeed. We didn't even make it all the way onto the bed, did we?"

"Close enough. Next time..."

"Next time," she whispered.

Dawn was just going to have to get used to it. For a while, at least.

~

THERE WERE no annoying customers in Dawn's Radiance on Tuesday. Were the people around her more well-behaved or was she the changed one? Did a long overdue orgasm really spark a shift in her personality?

Olive was happy. She was always pretty much *content* with her day-to-day life, but when was the last time she'd been genuinely *happy*? It had been a while.

She couldn't help but wonder if any of the neighbors had seen her run from Tuck's house to her own in the early morning hours, in her crumpled red dress, heels in hand. For the first time in her life she could actually say she'd taken the infamous *walk of shame*.

She felt no shame at all.

During business hours she talked to Mike a couple of times. Dawn and the baby boy were doing well. They'd probably head home tomorrow. She couldn't wait that long! Tonight she'd head to the maternity ward and visit with her sister. Maybe she could even hold the baby for a while. Dawn was sure to ask questions about Tuck, which Olive would either ignore or answer honestly. She hadn't decided.

If she'd been thinking she would've driven to work today instead of walking, but walking had become a habit, one she enjoyed. Her walk home after work was a brisk one. There was so much to do tonight!

Maybe Tuck would like to go to the hospital with her, to check out the results of his handiwork. Her heart dropped a little when she saw his empty driveway. Of course he was at work. Their schedules were so different it was a miracle they'd even met, much less...

Thank goodness he'd come over to say hello and save her from an unwanted Christmas tree.

She stripped off her work clothes and slipped into jeans, a casual blouse, and tennis shoes. What she'd worn all day had retail all over it, and she was glad to shed as much of it as she could. She didn't even think about her pirate ghost, not until she was in the midst of changing clothes.

Why should she care? If Giles was real, if he'd been hanging around watching for hundreds of years, then he'd seen countless naked people. In this house, since it was built. On the land before that. She wasn't special in that respect.

Before she left the house, she typed a quick text. *I'm going to the hospital to see Dawn and the baby. Did Mike tell you? They named the baby Nathaniel. If you want to stop by...*

She didn't want to come off as pushy, or needy, or desperate, so she deleted the last sentence. He knew where she'd be, and would stop by if it suited him.

She hit send and left the house in a bit of a hurry. So much to do! After a visit with her sister and nephew, she had another stop to make.

∼

STANDING behind the bar at The Magnolia, Tuck read Olive's text. He thought about responding. He thought about asking her if she wanted a ride to the hospital. He thought about saying a lot of things, but he did nothing.

He needed time to think, and when he was with Olive, he didn't.

Within a couple of days he'd found out he'd had a grandmother living down the road for years but it was too late to get to know her, since she'd died more than two years ago; he'd delivered a baby *again*, something that had not been on his list of experiences he wanted to repeat even though it had been kind of awesome; and he'd fallen for a woman who wasn't going to stay.

Olive had a life in Alabama, a good life from everything Mike had told him. A thriving business, friends, and her parents didn't live too far away. No man, to hear him tell it, not for years, so maybe she didn't need one.

He could relate. After a couple of earlier relationships went sour, he'd decided to be happy on his own for a while. He wanted to say the destruction of those relationships hadn't been his fault but looking back... maybe he'd been as much to blame as the women. Maybe it was all his fault. Maybe they'd just been wrong for him.

None of them had been anything like Olive.

Yesterday had been momentous. Dinner, a new baby, incredible sex. He liked Olive, he liked her a lot.

But like everyone else he'd ever cared about she wasn't going to stay, so why make more of this than it was or could ever be? Fun, for a while. Someone to spend Christmas with, and then she'd be gone. This holiday affair, if that's what it was, had begun with Olive saying she wasn't looking for a relationship. He saw more in them, or at least the possibility of more, but she was simply... hooking up. That should be fine with him; it should be perfect. So why was he mentally grousing about it now?

Olive was going to leave, too soon. She'd be back to visit, he supposed, and one day she'd show up with a husband on her arm. Kids would follow. Maybe she'd remember hooking up with him one Christmas with fondness.

Shit, he was thinking too much, overthinking everything. He liked her more than he'd expected he would, but neither of them needed the complication of a serious relationship.

She liked him, too; he knew it. That didn't mean she'd change her life for him. Whatever they had was temporary, a fling and nothing more.

The Magnolia stayed busy, even now as Christmas approached. Tuck wasn't the only one who didn't have family plans for Christmas. He wasn't the only one hiding from the holiday, just waiting for it to be over. He wondered if he could take his tree down this week, well before Christmas. He'd only put it up — well, he'd had it done — for Olive.

He was surprised to see Mike walk into The Magnolia on a Tuesday night. The new father had called several times today. Tuck always found a reason to send those calls to voicemail.

"He lives!" Mike said as he took a stool at the bar.

Unless he wanted to turn and run, there was no place to go. "Shouldn't you be at the hospital?"

"I should. If you'd answer your damn phone, I would be."

"Beer?"

Mike shook his head. "Not tonight. Though I will take a burger with the works, fries, and a glass of water."

Tuck put the order in, then returned to his friend. "So, Nathaniel," he said.

"Who told you? Olive, I guess. I wanted to tell you myself, but you didn't answer your damn phone."

"Don't you know how to text?"

"I thought this was too important to put in a text, but hell, what do I know. I hope you don't mind. No one calls you anything but Tuck, so it's not like it'll be confusing. Actually, I'm grateful. Dawn was planning to name him Edgar, after her grandfather. She moved that to the middle name, which suits me."

"It's fine. I've been Tuck for more than twenty years. And..." He grinned. "Edgar?"

"Yeah, that was a close one."

"You didn't have any say in the matter?"

Mike laughed. "Hell, no. You just wait. One day you'll understand."

He didn't think that day would ever come.

Mike demolished his burger and inhaled the fries. When he was done, he gave Tuck an odd, probing look.

"So, what's with you and Olive?"

The question of the day, one he had no answer for. Not for Mike, not for himself.

## CHAPTER 14

On Wednesday morning Olive thought about a walk on the beach, but the wind had picked up and it was a little chilly. She decided to stay in and work on her new project before it was time to head to the boutique.

She'd dropped the Walmart bags on the couch last night, before she'd gone to bed exhausted but happy. She was happier than she'd been in years, and why not? Tuck. Baby Nathaniel. A sister who hadn't yet forgiven her for sleeping with the man who'd delivered her baby, but would. It was the way of sisters.

Still in her pajamas, she dumped the contents of one bag onto the couch. The shoe ornament had called to her immediately, as she'd browsed the Christmas display. She did love a pretty shoe. The penguin was cute, and so was the snowman. She hung them, spaced appropriately, on her little tree.

She saved the ballerina for last. Her career hadn't gone the way she'd planned, but that time in her life had been important. Fun? No, not really. She'd been too focused on succeeding to enjoy it the way she should've. The dance was the thing. She should've simply enjoyed instead of being so determined to succeed, to be perfect, that she didn't see anything else.

She loved music. She loved to dance. So why didn't she?

"Stupid," she said as she hung the ballerina ornament front and center.

She leaned a little to the side to look at Tuck's truck through the window. The Ford was parked in his driveway, as it was every morning. He was home. He was right there, so close...

Should she call or text? Of course not. He worked late nights. He had to be sleeping, and it would be rude to wake him. Definitely rude. He hadn't responded to any of her texts yesterday, so maybe there was a crisis at work. Maybe he'd been busy and worked late and...

She didn't want to imagine that he might be blowing her off now that he'd slept with her. He wasn't one of those guys. Couldn't be. There was more than that between them, in a way she'd never expected.

It was windy outside, but there shouldn't be any wind in her living room! A faint breeze hit her square in the face. She'd think there was a draft, but this wind was warm. Not hot, not unpleasant. *Warm*, like a touch from another person.

Or a ghost.

"Okay, Giles, I get it," she said. "To be honest no one has ever used the word 'brave' to describe Olive Carson. I'm careful. I plan for every possibility. I'm analytical." *Usually*.

If she analyzed her relationship with Tuck, she'd have to admit that it was a temporary, fun escape from the holidays, from her carefully planned life. He was a vacation fling, a way to pass the time...

But that wasn't true, not entirely. There was more. She felt it, even if it didn't exactly make sense.

Olive looked down at the bags on her couch. She had a little more time before she needed to head to the boutique. Might as well be productive. She reached down and snagged the premade wreath with the slightly wonky red bow.

∼

BY THE TIME he got out of bed, Olive was gone. Dawn's Radiance would've been opened for a couple of hours by the time he woke. Her car wasn't in the driveway. With today's cooler than normal temps and that wind, it made sense that she'd drive.

He didn't want to knock around the house with nothing to do, not when his mind was spinning. Might as well head to work. There was always something to do at The Magnolia.

Tuck headed for his pickup but was distracted by something on Olive's front porch. He walked to the sidewalk to get a better look, stopped, and stared.

A wreath hung on her front door. Greenery, bells, a red ribbon at the bottom. Every time she opened her door, those bells would jingle. There was something in the window, too. He moved down the sidewalk to get a better look. Gnomes. A Christmas gnome in red and green had been placed in each of the front windows.

She'd come here hating Christmas, or at least merely tolerating it. Now she was taking the time to decorate a rental. Was it because of her family? Had her nieces given her more holiday gifts she felt obligated to put to use?

Was he having an effect on her holiday outlook? She'd sure as hell changed his.

He headed for his truck. Nah. Getting laid had put her in a good mood, that was all. Any man would've had the same effect. Woman were emotional; they always made more of sex than was necessary.

Did he like her? He did.

Would he change his life for her? No, he wasn't changing for anyone.

Did he still want a dance for Christmas?

Hell no. At this point a dance with Olive would be much too dangerous.

~

It was an oddly slow Wednesday, so Olive didn't mind closing the boutique for a quick lunch break. The wind had died down, so she walked. Man, she was going to miss walking everywhere when she went home! Traffic on 280 was a nightmare most days, and she couldn't go anywhere without getting on that busy road.

As she walked away from the boutique, she noticed a vacant space. Like the boutique it was in one of the strip centers rather than in an old house. A *For Lease* sign hung in the window. Olive stopped to look. She held her hands up to the glass to mute the glare from the sun so she could see inside. Nothing had been left behind from the previous tenant. Beyond the window was a simple, empty, square space, which reminded her of her first dance studio. It would also make a nice office, if she decided to expand her event planning business. There probably weren't enough local events to keep her busy, but if she could draw in folks from Biloxi...

She jerked away from the window. What was she thinking? She had no intention of moving to Seawolf Beach. This was just a visit. A vacation. A temporary...

Temporary what? Escape. Adventure. Happiness.

Happiness shouldn't be temporary.

She continued on, walking briskly. She wasn't hungry, but coffee would be nice. Put enough sugar and creamer in it and a cup would qualify as a meal, right?

Hart's Vinyl Depot sold excellent coffee.

There wasn't much of a crowd in the depot, so maybe it was just a slow day all across town, not just in the boutique. Anna busied herself cleaning behind the coffee bar. Colt was nowhere to be seen, but he was probably around. Somewhere. Talking to Maude? Talking to another of the ghosts who inhabited this haunted depot?

She'd love to have a nice, long chat with him, but at the same time she wasn't sure she wanted to know more than she already did. So many questions...

Anna smiled and offered a friendly hello. She was probably just happy to have a customer on this slow day.

Olive ordered coffee; Anna prepared it; Olive paid. So, now what?

Instead of walking out the door or moving to one of the benches near the coffee bar, Olive took a deep breath and looked into Anna's eyes.

"You're right. Tuck and I are... dating."

"I knew it." Anna grinned widely. "I'm glad. Tuck is a great guy, but he needs a good woman in his life."

Olive wanted to ask... *Why? Were there bad women in his past? Was there a deficit she needed to know about? What was wrong with him?* In her opinion nothing, but she couldn't say she knew him well.

For the past eight years she'd approached every man with that question, either in the back of her mind or on her lips. *What was wrong with him?* Something had to be. What was it?

"I'm not going to be around much longer," Olive said. Anna's smile faded. "But while I am here I want to help him, if I can. This thing with his grandmother..." She stopped speaking and swatted at the back of her neck. Were there mosquitos in the depot? Flies, maybe?

Anna held up her hands as if in surrender. "Maude, stop it. I know that's you. Leave Olive alone!"

Olive backed up and spun around, but of course she saw

nothing. She waited for another tickle on the back of her neck that never came.

Why was she tiptoeing around the issue? "I have a ghost in my house, my niece sees them, and Tuck is spun up about this grandmother issue. I can live with the first two, since I won't be here much longer, but while I'm in Seawolf Beach I want to help him. Tell me more about these pearl earrings. Tell me everything."

~

A GOOD DUMPSTER fire was just what Tuck needed to get his mind into a better place. A different place, anyway. The call had gone out and he'd gladly left Ginny behind the bar. In the back parking lot he'd pulled on the firefighter rig he always kept in the back of his truck, and then he'd joined the rest of the volunteer crew and the firetruck behind a new restaurant on the highway, not far from The Magnolia. For a while he focused on the job at hand.

Which sadly didn't take long enough to provide much in the way of mental relief.

He invited the rest of the crew to The Magnolia for a round on the house. About half of them accepted. The rest, Mike included, declined. They wanted or needed to go home. Maybe they'd just eaten. Could be dinner was waiting for him. Wives, kids, parents waited for them.

No one waited for Tuck. He'd never minded that fact so much before Olive had come crashing into his life. No, she hadn't crashed. She was more subtle than that. She'd slipped in, she'd snuck into his life when he hadn't been looking. There was no way he could've been prepared for her.

She made him long for more, for family and dinner waiting

for him at the end of the day, for a woman in his bed who wouldn't be gone the next morning. These thoughts had crossed his mind in the past, of course they had, but he'd never felt them so deeply. Nate Tucker didn't do deep feelings. He floated along through life on his own and content. He had a booming business, a great house, plenty of friends. He'd delivered not one but two babies.

He could do without that happening again, but he did love having a great story to tell. That's all this Christmas thing with Olive was. A great story.

One he had no intention of ever telling anyone.

She made him want more.

She terrified him, because he'd never wanted *more* so much that it was painful.

How did she know he was thinking about her? The text came in as he walked into his office to grab a change of clothes. He smelled like smoke.

*Busy?*

*A little. What's up?*

*Thinking about you. When will you be home?*

He could leave the bar in Ginny's hands, go home, and ask Olive if she'd like to come over to his place and take a shower with him. She'd say yes, he knew it. He'd never get over her if he got in any deeper. Wanting more was a trap. Normally he'd be thrilled that there was no chance a former lover would be waiting around the next corner, or might come into the bar after whatever they had was over either with a new fella or to check on him. This would normally be the perfect situation for him. Love 'em and leave 'em. Always. Anything else was foolish.

*Probably by three a.m.*

Her response began with a laughing emoji. *Too late for me, I'm afraid. Maybe I'll see you tomorrow.*

*Maybe. Night, Olive.*

*Night.*

That ended the text conversation.

He thought about starting it back up again with a quickly typed *I'll be right there*.

But he didn't. Olive could break his heart if he let it happen. Something about her... something he couldn't grasp... made him want what he couldn't have more intensely than ever.

He could love her. Love didn't last.

# CHAPTER 15

Old folks' homes were creepy, in Olive's opinion. Not that anyone here called this place or others like it an old folks' home. They were retirement villages, or senior apartments, or something along those lines.

She steeled her spine and walked into the dining room, which was filled with, well, old folks.

When she'd texted Tuck last night, he'd blown her off. She could do the same here; she could refuse to do what Anna and Colt had asked her to do and move on with her life.

If she'd refused, Anna probably would've given it a shot. Anna, or Colt, or both. But they had to live here, after the deed was done. Their involvement, the questions they would ask, might stir up too many questions. Since Olive wouldn't be here long, since she and Tuck were dating, or something like that, they thought her involvement was more logical. Maybe it was. Maybe they were cowards.

She'd be in town for another week, maybe a day or two longer. She didn't need a man; she wasn't looking for romance. Her sister would help her pass the time. Nieces and a new nephew needed to be cuddled. Her parents would be here in two days. She could easily get lost in what remained of the holiday season and forget what had happened with Tuck.

He'd been a bump in the road, not much more than a one-night stand.

But she liked him, he'd helped her find a way to enjoy Christmas again, and whether or not she ever saw him again... this was important. At least, Colt seemed to think so. No, *Maude* seemed to think so.

Once she took care of this, she'd have an excuse to call Tuck or stop by his house. If she got anywhere with this chore. If Maude was right.

Holy cow, she'd been sent on an errand by a ghost.

The dining room was small, which made sense. Seawolf Beach wasn't a big town; they didn't need a huge retirement home. Olive moved to the center of the room and raised her voice to ask, "Is Betty here?"

Two women looked her way. She didn't have a last name, and she hadn't expected there to be more than one Betty. "I'm looking for the Betty who was friends with Maude Reeves. Wait, Reeves was her maiden name, not her married name, if that helps."

One Betty returned to her meal; the other stood. "Maude and I were great friends."

"I hate to disturb your lunch," Olive said as she walked toward the woman, "but I only have a little bit of time before I have to get back to work." She didn't like taking a long break when the boutique was so busy, but this had to be done.

It had taken her hours to come up with an excuse other than *a ghost sent me...* "A letter was recently found in Maude's belongings."

"Did her son find it? The eldest, I expect. He certainly took his time going through her things." She gave a huff of disapproval.

"Yes, her son," Olive said. It was simpler to just agree and move on. "There was a mention of pearl earrings Maude wanted to go to... her grandson. She seemed to think you might have them."

Betty visibly paled. Her eyes darted to the side and one hand trembled. "I'm finished with my lunch. Walk to my room with me."

She nodded to her companions and stepped away from the table. Olive wanted to run but she had to let Betty, who did not run, set the pace as they walked into the lobby and to the elevator. The woman didn't say a word until they were in the elevator with the door closed.

"I borrowed the earrings just a week or so before Maude passed. I had a date with Joseph, and I didn't think Maude would miss the earrings so quickly. Naturally she missed them right away. I didn't realize she held those pearls in her hands every night before she went to bed, that she cherished them so much. She was so upset, I was afraid to tell her I'd borrowed them. I did plan to return them, when an opportunity arose, but then she was gone."

The slow elevator took them to the second floor. Betty walked to the second door on the right and opened it wide.

"I'm sure she'd understand," Olive said. Her palms were sweating, she was so nervous. And, well, the apartment felt like the heat was set to eighty degrees.

Betty laughed. "I loved Maude, I did, but she wasn't always understanding. I couldn't tell her the truth, and I was afraid to tell anyone what I'd done after she was gone because I was afraid they'd blame me. Did I bring on Maude's heart attack because I upset her?"

"Oh no. I'm sure that's not the case." She wasn't *sure*, but it seemed like the thing to say.

The apartment was simply laid out. A main room with a

couch and television; a kitchenette which looked to be rarely used; a bathroom and bedroom. Betty walked into the bedroom and to her dresser. She opened a small jewelry box and there they were, the infamous earrings that kept a ghost earthbound, if Colt was to be believed. The pearl earrings were simple, small, and were what her own grandmother had always called ear clips. When these had been made, pierced ears weren't at all common so when worn they were attacked to the earlobes with sturdy clips. Betty removed the earrings from the box and placed them in Olive's hands.

"These are your responsibility now. My heart feels lighter already. I've worried about these so, but I was also afraid to say anything. Afraid her family would brand me a thief, or worse, accuse me of killing Maude, of bringing on her heart attack. I don't want to be kicked out of my home." She looked Olive in the eye. "Did you know about Phillip? I admit, I wondered if her family even knew about these earrings."

Phillip. Tuck's grandfather. Maude's secret love, all these years. "I know a little. Did Maude talk about him?"

"Not often, but on Taco Tuesday, when they served margaritas, she opened up quite a bit." Betty laughed at the memory. "Maude had a family who loved her, she had a great life, but she always carried Phillip and their daughter in her heart."

Olive grasped the earrings in one hand, placing the other hand on Betty's arm. "These earrings will go to that daughter's son."

Tears bloomed in Betty's eyes. "Oh, I'm so glad. It's right, isn't it?"

"Yes it is." Now she just had to find a way to tell Tuck…

∽

Every time he looked at Olive's house, he noticed another Christmas doodad she'd added to the front porch. He wouldn't be surprised to find an inflatable Santa in her yard early one morning when he pulled into his driveway.

This morning there were lights. Tiny, colorful lights were strung across the banister. Tuck stopped beside his truck to study her work. To be honest it looked like a trained monkey, more likely an untrained one, had strung those lights. They were bunched in one place, hanging crookedly in another, and instead of going up and over to the other side of the porch, they ran across the top step.

Was this a test? Did she know he'd be compelled to fix the messy lights?

After two in the morning she'd be sound asleep. He was still wound up from a busy night at The Magnolia so sleep wasn't in his immediate future. There were plenty of nights he didn't get to sleep until sunrise, and with Olive on his mind this was bound to be one of those nights.

Tuck crossed into Olive's yard without making a sound. If the lights had been on the edge of the roof he'd never be able to fix the mess without making a lot of racket. He was glad to know she hadn't gotten on a ladder to decorate, and just as glad to be able to fix this sad attempt.

As if he'd ever cared about Christmas decorations before. Olive cared, and that was all that mattered.

He worked slowly, quietly, starting at one end and working his way across. Untangling, reattaching the cord to the banister, lifting it off the step and up. She'd done it all wrong, but mentally picturing Olive taking on this job made him smile. She'd definitely done it on her own. If she'd asked for her brother-in-law's help, Mike would've done a decent job.

He was almost finished when he heard a creak. The front door opened a crack. Just a crack, no more. On the other side of the narrow space one eye watched him. One deep brown, inquisitive eye.

"Don't you know better than to open the door in the middle of the night?" he asked.

"I knew it was you," she whispered.

"How did you know?"

"Who else would fix my decorating disaster at three a.m.?" The door opened a little wider. "Besides, I looked out the window to be sure. Want a cup of coffee or something?"

"No thanks. You should get back to bed."

"I should," she said. "So should you."

He'd been avoiding her for days because he knew he couldn't resist that kind of invitation...

Tuck walked toward the door. She opened it wide. Olive Carson stood there in rumpled Christmas pajamas that did *not* scream seduction. Her dark hair was messy; her feet were bare.

He'd never seen anything sexier.

"If I come in there will be no coffee. You know that."

"I do." She stepped back, asking him in.

"I'm trying to quit you," he admitted as he approached her.

"I kinda figured that might be the case. Care to tell me why?"

"Not at the moment, no."

She backed up; he went inside and closed the door behind him. The light from the hallway was dim, but he could see enough to note the changes. "It looks like Santa threw up in your living room."

She laughed a little, moved toward and into him, and draped her arms around his neck. "I've missed you."

That was all it took. She squealed when he picked her up and carried her toward the back of the house and her bedroom. Her bed. His surrender.

∽

"I LURED YOU IN," Olive said as Tuck dropped her onto the bed. She'd heard movement on the front porch and had suspected it might be him. No, she'd *known* it was him. "Stringing Christmas lights is harder than it looks."

"You could've asked for help."

"You weren't here, and Mike has his hands full. Who else am I going to ask? Besides..." Might as well confess. "I knew you'd be compelled to fix it for me, that my sad attempt would lure you to my front door."

"You're a wily woman," he said as he started to undress.

"No one has ever called me wily before." She stretched out across the bed, waiting for him, waiting for this man who'd come roaring into her life to turn it upside down.

She didn't want to think about ghosts, grandmothers, or where she'd be two weeks from now. No one had ever accused Olive of being a live-in-the-moment person, but right now that's all she wanted. To live in the moment. To enjoy whatever this was while it lasted.

Whatever this was. Love? Lust for sure, but was it more? Was this hormones or heart? "Stop thinking," she whispered. "Just feel."

"What?" Tuck said as he joined her on the bed and began to undress her. He spent a lovely moment caressing her breasts as he removed the pajama top.

"I said I should be wily more often."

He made quick work of her pajama bottoms, and then he was there. Touching her everywhere, making her forget everything. Everything but this. Touch, a driving need, a closeness that went beyond the physical, Tuck's warmth, her racing heartbeat. The world spun just for them.

When she couldn't stand to wait another second, he was there. Inside her. A part of her. There was truly nothing and no one else in the world but the two of them and the release they offered one another.

His skin against hers was heavenly. Their bodies joined and moved and danced, yes *danced*, until the sensation they created went beyond anything she'd ever known or expected.

She shattered; he came with her.

Everything slowed. Their bodies; her mind and heart.

When he kissed her it was slow, easy, as natural as breathing. Was it foolish to think this was love when she was still reeling from sex? She'd ask herself that question again in the morning.

When they'd been kissing on the couch and there hadn't been a condom handy, she'd been able to control herself. She'd convinced herself that she possessed self-control where Nate Tucker was concerned. That was, apparently, no longer the case.

She hadn't given the earrings that sat in her dresser drawer a thought as he'd come inside her house, as he'd come into her bed. This wasn't a night for ghosts, family secrets, or confessions. The night was just for them.

"That was... unexpected," Tuck said as he moved away.

"Was it?"

"For me, yes. For you? I'm shocked. You seduced me, Olive Carson."

"With badly hung Christmas lights and holiday pajamas."

He didn't respond right away.

"I've never seduced anyone before," she whispered.

"Why not?"

"I never wanted any man as much as I want you."

After a long moment he muttered something. She must've misheard. It sounded like he said, "You terrify me."

## CHAPTER 16

Tuck woke in a bed that was not his own. It took him a moment to remember where he was and how he'd gotten here. *Olive.* Damn, he hadn't seen her coming.

No matter where he went from here, this Christmas had changed his life. There had been no other season like it. Thanks to the good and the bad, a lot of uncertainty, eye-opening moments... he was not entirely the same man he'd been a few weeks ago. Where would he go from here?

Colt's news, if he chose to believe it, was life shattering in itself. Should he pursue what might be... *might be*... a new extended family? There could be family reunions. Cousins. Aunts and uncles. Thanksgiving and Christmas celebrations with too many people and too much food. Were there relatives with blue eyes and the same nose Tuck saw in the mirror? Would he see his own traits in others?

The only blood relative he'd ever known had been Uncle Houston, a man with a questionable past and colorful cohorts. Was his mother's side of the family respectable? Were they kind, like Doreen Tucker?

Whatever he did with the information Colt had passed on, if

he did anything at all, would have to wait. He wasn't about to show up with his claims during the holidays. Maybe after the first of the year. Summer. Next Christmas. *Never*.

Then there was Olive, who'd turned his life upside down as much as this granny news. He liked her too much. He cared about her in a way he hadn't cared for anything or anyone in a very long time. He liked being alone. His life was safer that way. Keep it simple, that was his motto. Olive was anything but simple, and even if he did care about her what difference did it make? She wasn't going to stay.

She made him think about the things he craved most and at the same time was frightened of. A family of his own. A connection that went so deep it would never be broken. A woman he could call his own, children, a home that no one could ever take away. When he looked at Olive, when he lost himself in her, that's what he saw. What he craved.

He wanted to ask her to stay, but when she said no it would break his heart. Nate Tucker didn't do broken hearts. Maybe he'd broken a few along the way, but his own heart was immune.

Or had been.

Olive would only be here for a few more days. After Christmas she'd be back to her life. A life that didn't include him.

The same way his life didn't include her.

He crawled out of bed and grabbed his clothes off the floor, glancing at the bedside clock as he started to dress. It was noon. Olive had been at work for at least a couple of hours. She'd left him sleeping. A vague, half-sleep memory crept into his brain. She'd kissed him on the cheek and pulled the covers over his shoulder. Maybe she'd said something, but he couldn't remember what.

As he walked into the living room, he had a chance to study all the new Christmas decorations. For someone who claimed to hate the holiday, Olive had gone all out. There were even snowflake pillows on the couch; a gnome similar to the ones in the windows sitting on the coffee table; a kitchen towel with snowmen on it tossed over the back of a chair. When she loaded up her car to go home, it would be packed to the headliner.

He saw the ballerina ornament last. It caught his eye, caused him to stop in his tracks. Olive didn't have fond memories of her time as a dancer. In fact, it had scarred her in a way that made it difficult to think or talk about. So why the new ornament? Why the reminder? She'd said this Christmas was *nice*, and he'd like to think he'd had something to do with that shift in her attitude.

Like it made a difference.

His phone buzzed as he left the ballerina behind and walked toward the front door. Emergency? Colt? Or Olive?

*You up?*

*Barely. On my way home.*

*My mom just called. She and Dad are coming in tonight instead of tomorrow. I'll be at Dawn's until late. Catch you after?*

Tuck hesitated. This was sounding too much like he and Olive were an actual couple, making plans for the night, making plans around her family. The sex was great, but this was more than that. Wasn't it?

*Maybe. I'll have to work late.*

*That's fine. Later.*

In his experience, any woman who said *that's fine* wasn't fine at all.

He could enjoy Olive while she was here, knowing it wouldn't last, or he could end it now and save what was left of his soul before she shattered it.

*Later.*

Decisions would have to wait. When Olive was nothing more than a text it was easy to decide to end the relationship while he was ahead. When he saw her, if he saw her... that would be a different story.

~

She should be happy her folks had decided to push on through and get to their grandkids, including their new grandson, a day early. Still, she would've been glad to have one more night with Tuck before family obligations ruined everything.

No, not *ruined*. Interfered.

Though Tuck had said he had to work tonight. Maybe her parents' early arrival didn't make a bit of difference. She'd be home eventually, and so would he. Who needed sleep? She still had to talk to him about the earrings, hand them over to him, but how? When? The story Colt had shared wasn't welcome news for Tuck. He likely wouldn't want a physical reminder to deal with.

Still, she'd promised. Colt. Anna. Maude. She'd given them her word. Yes, she'd made a promise to a ghost.

Tonight was for family. Ghosts, earrings, and the unexpected possibility that she loved Tuck could wait.

Ava was so excited to see her grandparents and all the brightly wrapped presents they placed beneath the huge Christmas tree, she didn't seem at all distracted by Rosaline or any other spirits. Willow was, as usual, not as loud or active as her sister, but when she had the chance she jumped into her grandfather's lap and snuggled there.

Olive thought her heart would break at the sight. She'd never really wanted children, even though she loved her nieces and her new nephew, but she'd never before felt so completely encompassed in love, family... and the idea of one day having all that for herself.

She took her mom a glass of water and a cookie, then sat

beside her. Nathaniel slept, snug in her arms. Well, arm. Grammy Carson knew how to hold a baby and have a free hand to function. "So," she said. "Tell me about this Tuck." Before Olive had a chance to respond, her mother added, "Such an odd name for a grown man."

*If you think his name is odd, what will you think when we start talking about ghosts?* She didn't go there.

"Who told you about Tuck?" And *what* had they told?

"Dawn, of course. She was upset for a time that you were dating the man who delivered Nathaniel, but I think she's come to terms with it. I don't know what her problem was."

Not going there.

"It sounds as if he did an adequate job. Dawn and Nathaniel are both healthy and happy."

"He'd delivered a baby before."

"So I heard." She shifted the baby a little, bounced him lightly when he started to squirm. "I didn't expect you'd find a man in Seawolf Beach. How inconvenient. It's not like you're going to be here much longer, and even with the best of intentions a long-distance relationship never works. I suppose a little distraction during the holidays isn't a bad thing, not for a woman your age."

"Mom!"

"I'm a realist, Olive. You're thirty years old. I don't want to see you alone for the rest of your life because one selfish, clumsy oaf..." She took a deep breath and looked her youngest daughter in the eye. "I don't like to talk about that man. Yes, he injured your hip, but he did more than that. He destroyed your trust in men. Some don't deserve trust, but many men are perfectly acceptable and trustworthy. And let's face it," she said in a lowered voice. "They do have their... uses. If this Tuck helps you move on, then who am I to question his silly name?"

"Mom, you talk too much."

"So I've been told."

"But you're not wrong."

Her mom's response, "You usually hate that about me," was followed by a sly wink.

Olive stood, stretched, and said her goodbyes. Dawn was surprised she was leaving so early, but Olive told a half truth. She hadn't slept well last night. Let them assume she was going home to fall into bed and sleep.

She did need to stop by the Jasmine Street house, but sleep was not on her mind.

## CHAPTER 17

He should've expected Olive to show up after last night. Well, this morning. A fantastic, foolish, life-changing morning. But he hadn't been looking for her at all. No, he'd gotten lost in the routine of working at the bar and allowed himself to put her out of his mind for a while. He turned around and there she was, walking through the main entrance of The Magnolia, looking as out of place as she had the last time she'd surprised him by stopping by.

Seeing her here only reinforced his opinion that their worlds were too far apart to ever merge in any way other than the physical. The physical was great; it was different from anything he'd known. But that didn't change the facts.

She wasn't for him.

"Everything okay?" he asked as she approached him and took an empty stool.

"Okayish," she said.

He grunted a little. "What can I get you?"

"Nothing. I have to be able to drive home tonight, and we both know what happened last time I was here."

The band had been between sets when she'd walked in, but

they were gathering on the stage again. It was about to get too loud for him to hear her. Maybe that was a good thing.

She glanced toward the stage, then up and down the bar. "Is there a place we can talk? Privately?"

Ginny had everything well in hand. There was no reason for him to say no. No reason other than he had zero control when he was alone with her. What could he say?

"Sure. My office." He walked to the end of the bar. She left her stool and met him there. "Okayish, huh?"

Olive sighed. "For so many reasons. My parents are here. Tomorrow is going to be crazy at the boutique. And…" She hesitated as he opened the door to his office and let her walk inside. "Monday will be my last day there. We'll be closed Christmas Eve. A couple of weeks ago I was spun up about difficult customers and now…" She laughed a little. "I'm going to miss retail." She glanced around the neat, organized space. "It looks like you keep your books on the computer?"

"Doesn't everyone?"

"Not Dawn. She insists…" Her smile faded. She looked at him with those dark brown eyes that did him in. He saw her uncertainty. "I'm not here to talk about Dawn's Radiance, customers, or accounting systems."

Of course not. "Why are you here?"

She stepped behind him and closed the door, muffling the sound of voices, the clink of glasses, and the band as they started up. "I should've done this last night, but I didn't want to ruin the moment. Then this morning you were sleeping so soundly, I couldn't wake you. I thought maybe we'd see each other tonight, but then Mom and Dad came in and, well…"

He saved her as best he could. "Olive, say what you have to say."

She placed her purse on his desk, opened it, reached inside, and came out with a small, gray, velvety bag with a drawstring. "I know you don't want to talk about Maude."

"No, I don't."

"But Anna and Colt asked me if I'd help, and I couldn't say no."

"My ghostly grandmother, if that's what she is, is none of your business." His words were sharp and intentionally hurtful. He just wanted her to stop, to go away, to leave him in peace.

He saw the hurt in her expression. "I suppose that's true, but here I am poking my nose in where it doesn't belong because I care about you and this is important."

"Don't," he said.

"Don't poke my nose in your business or don't care?"

"Both."

That should send her packing, but it didn't.

"I'll be out of your hair soon, I promise, but this isn't mine to keep." She dumped the contents of the bag onto her palm. "These are the earrings your grandfather, Phillip, gave to Maude not long before he died. She wants you to have them."

"No." A simple no should be enough, but it wasn't.

"She wants you to have them so..." Olive hesitated, looked away, took a deep breath. "So one day you can give them to the woman you love."

*That would never happen.*

"I don't want those crappy old earrings."

"Take them anyway," she insisted. "Then I can go to the depot, tell Maude... well, tell Colt to tell Maude, if that's what it takes... they're in your hands. Maybe then she'll move on to where she's supposed to be."

"You've certainly embraced this woo-woo ghostly crap."

"What choice do I have? The ghost crap is right there under my nose. It's in my house, in Dawn's house, and while I don't see or hear anything like Colt and Ava, the evidence is pretty damn incontrovertible."

He wanted to argue with her, but nothing coherent popped into his mind. "What if I don't want a granny ghost? What if I want to go back to a time when I had no idea ghosts even existed? Colt is crazy. Kids have vivid imaginations. Why isn't that enough?"

"Because it's not."

The earrings on her palm were old and probably worthless. No one wore earrings with those clips that looked as if they'd be painful. They probably weren't real pearls but some kind of fake shit. He didn't want them, but Olive wasn't going to leave until he did. "Put them on the desk."

"You can't even touch these earrings long enough to take them from my hand?"

*I can't.* "I don't want to break them."

Olive returned the earrings to the bag, closed it snuggly, and placed the bag on his desk. He'd toss them in the dumpster later.

"Sorry if I upset you," she said.

"You didn't."

"Maybe I haven't known you for very long, but I know that look. I'm not sure if I should call it upset or angry, but you're not *right*. You're not the Tuck I know and... well, know."

Know and love? He couldn't go there.

"Will I see you later?" she asked.

It was tempting. She'd be here a few more days, and the sex was great. If he could get past the fact that they had no future he could be with her again, and again, and maybe again. "No, sorry. I'm super busy tonight, and will be all weekend. I didn't get enough sleep last night, so when I get home I should really..."

"You don't need to over-explain," she said. "I get it. See you Christmas Eve? Mike said he invited you to their party." She looked him dead in the eye. "Don't bother to answer. Judging by the look on your face, I'm guessing you'll be busy here." Instead of running she stepped closer, went up on her toes, and gave him a quick kiss. As she stepped back she said, "You made this Christmas... Christmas again. I appreciate that. Thanks for making me braver than I've been in years."

She left his office without looking back. He should follow her and apologize for being an ass, but he didn't. He wasn't nearly as brave as she was.

∽

ANNA WAS EXPECTING HER, since Olive had texted on her way over. It was going to be a busy day for both of them since this was the last Saturday before Christmas, so best to get this taken care of before the long day of retail began. She heard the door unlock as she approached, watched as it swung open. Anna invited her in and re-locked the door behind her.

"Coffee?" Anna asked.

"I never say no to coffee."

They both walked toward the coffee bar, Anna heading to the coffee maker, Olive making herself comfortable on the customer side. She reached into her purse, but Anna waved her off. "On the house. You've helped us out so much, I say you get free coffee for life."

"I might take you up on that."

Anna made two cups — sweet and light for Olive, black for herself — and carried them around the bar. She handed one cup to Olive then sat on the old, long, wooden bench. Olive sat beside her.

"How did it go?" she asked.

This is why she was here, right? Best to keep it simple. "I retrieved the earrings from Betty, who is very sorry about the mixup, on Thursday, and I handed them over to Tuck last night."

"How did he take it?"

Olive took a long sip. The coffee was almost too hot, but she wanted a moment to choose her words. The point of all this was to help Maude move on. The truth might not help at all. But... she couldn't lie. Not about this. "Not well, I'm afraid. He's having a hard time accepting..." Ghosts, grandmothers, *her*. "Well, everything."

Anna didn't seem surprised or upset. "You don't seem to be having an issue with any of it."

"I don't, which is really weird. It doesn't make sense, but I'm different here." Bolder, braver, more open than she'd been in years. "A few weeks ago if you'd said *ghost* to me, I would've been out of here like a shot." *Love* might've gotten the same response.

Anna was an observer. It would be tough to get anything past her. "You care about Tuck."

"I do, but I'm afraid he doesn't care about me at all." As she said the words she knew they weren't true. At least, not entirely. She'd guarded her heart for years. Tuck had all but locked his behind a brick wall. "Tell me more about Maude."

Anna took a sip of her coffee, then said, "I only know what Colt tells me. She's sweet, loves to dance, talks a lot, and until all this happened he had no idea why she was stuck here. Lately she's been driving him crazy. Now that you've handed the earrings over to Tuck maybe she'll move on. Or at least stop hounding Colt at all hours."

"I can't believe that I actually believe all of this," Olive said, smiling.

"You know what's weird?" Anna asked in a lowered voice.

"There's more?"

"Since I moved in here, I find myself occasionally using an old-fashioned word. Now and then I crave banana pudding, which I really didn't care for before a couple of months ago. I'm a songwriter, and for the past two months I've been obsessed with the idea of writing one about pearl earrings."

"I'd love to hear it!"

"It's not done, because the story isn't over."

She thought of Tuck and the way he'd looked at the pearls as if they were a coiled snake. When would this story be done? Another thought crept in. "So you're telling me ghosts can affect the people around them? That even if you can't see or hear them, they might slip into your head somehow?"

"Colt says he doesn't know, and he's not sure how he can research the idea. But with me and Maude…" She shrugged. "Maybe."

Olive took another long swig of her coffee, draining the disposable cup. "Could living with a fearless pirate somehow make me more willing to take risks?" To be bold, brave, fearless.

Anna laughed a little. "Who knows?"

That was the story of this trip to Seawolf Beach. *Who knows?*

# CHAPTER 18

Tuck had done his best to avoid running into his neighbor for the past few days. *Coward*. She was gone when he went to work and sleeping when he got home. If he occasionally glanced toward the blue house and wondered what she was doing, if she was sleeping soundly, if she dreamed of him. He quickly shook those thoughts off.

He should've made himself clear Friday night. He could've told her they were too different, that he wanted more, that she terrified him because when he allowed it he was certain he could have *more* with her.

When a man looked at a woman like Olive, he shouldn't feel fear.

Christmas Eve had finally arrived. The elder Carsons had settled in. They'd be here for the next several days, doting on their grandchildren and their daughters, celebrating the holiday with family. The rest of this week and next, with the busy season over, the boutique would be closed. After that it would be Dawn's problem, he supposed. She could hire part-time help or go back to work herself, though it seemed too soon to him. What did he know about new mothers?

Nothing. Nothing at all.

He'd agreed to stop by the Woodward house for their annual Christmas Eve shindig weeks ago. Before he'd gotten involved with Olive, before he'd delivered Dawn's baby, before he'd found out about Maude. He could just skip the thing, come up with an excuse, and spend the night at The Magnolia with all the other losers.

The problem was, he didn't feel like a loser. It didn't make any sense at all, but he wanted to see Olive before she left town. He needed to be sure that whatever they had was well and truly done.

It should be. But for some odd reason he had *hope*.

With so many people at the party, there wouldn't be much parking. He walked from his house, taking slow, long strides, wondering with each step if he'd change his mind and turn back before he got to Mike's house. He didn't turn back; he didn't stop. He continued to move forward, one steady step after another.

He wanted to see Olive one last time. He needed to be sure. Something perverse inside him wanted that glimmer of hope to survive, maybe even to grow.

He stopped on the sidewalk in front of the Woodward house. Even though he'd made it this far, turning back remained an option. The street was crowded with cars, as he'd known it would be. Through the big front window a huge Christmas tree with colorful lights twinkled. Beyond that tree were people, standing and talking, walking past, laughing. Even with his limited view he saw more than one ugly holiday sweater.

He'd been a soldier, years ago. He'd fought fires and delivered not one but two babies in stressful situations. But this... this was terrifying.

The front door opened, and Olive stepped onto the front porch. She closed the door behind her. "I thought that was you."

*Too late to run.*

Tuck took a deep breath and walked to the porch. "Just catching my breath before I joined the chaos."

She laughed. It was nice. "Well, come on in. We've been waiting for you."

*We?*

Inside the chaos was real. Some of Mike and Dawn's friends also had children, and they all seemed to be of an age where running and screeching was their default. All four grandparents were gathered around baby Nathaniel at the moment. The kid slept through the noise and background Christmas music, something old and mellow that sounded like Andy Williams, without a care in the world.

The last time he'd seen the kid, Nathaniel hadn't been so clean and comfortable.

As he surveyed the crowd, Olive slipped away. Great. She didn't want to be near him. He couldn't blame her, not after the way he'd acted Friday night. Tuck said hello to a couple of guys he knew from the volunteer fire department, already wondering how long he had to stay, wondering even harder why he'd bothered to come.

Before he could come up with an excuse to leave, Olive, standing at the foot of the stairway, cleared her throat. At her direction, Mike stopped Andy Williams. He removed one record and replaced it with another, pausing with the turntable arm grasped between two fingers, waiting before starting the new music.

"Ladies and gentlemen," Olive began. "I give you the Sugar Plum Fairies." She nodded and stepped down and out of the way.

Mike lowered the arm to play classical music Tuck recognized but could not name. Ava and Willow, dressed in colorful fairy costumes, danced down the stairs to a small section of floor space Olive had cleared for them.

They danced. Not well, but with enthusiasm and vigor. There were a few ballet moves in there, he recognized that much. Olive stood nearby and occasionally offered silent direction. Waving her hands, squaring her shoulders, reminding the girls of their steps when they forgot. The dance was sloppy, imperfect, and utterly charming.

Twice during the performance Olive looked his way and caught his eye. To make sure he hadn't bolted? Would she chase him down if he did?

She'd hidden from Christmas for years, she'd been hurt. But this year she had a ballerina ornament on her little tree. She'd taught her nieces a dance. And she smiled through it all.

How could he let her go? How could he allow Olive to walk away? She was special. She was *his*. He'd known it all along.

When the show was over to tremendous applause, Olive hugged the girls, then headed his way. "They wanted to wait for you," she said.

"You taught them, I guess," he said.

"I did. It was more fun than I expected. I honestly didn't think I had any love for ballet left in me, but... I do." She took his hand and led him away from the tree, toward the kitchen.

When they passed Dawn, who sat in an easy chair, the new mother glared at them. "I told you..." she whispered.

"Too late, sister," Olive said with a smile.

Dawn rolled her eyes, but she also grinned. *Sister stuff?*

"What was that about?" Tuck asked.

"It's not important. She'll get over it." The kitchen was deserted, which seemed to be what Olive was looking for. She turned to face him. "I have something for you."

She reached into the pocket of her Christmasy dress and pulled out a folded envelope.

"You can open this if you want to, or not. That's your choice. But I couldn't help myself. I had to do a little digging online."

He knew what was in that envelope. Relatives. Maybe an uncle with his nose or a cousin who also couldn't stand cilantro.

His simple life was about to change, in so many ways. "If I decide to contact them, will you..."

"Hold your hand? You bet I will."

He stuffed the envelope into his jeans pocket. "I was an ass Friday," he said. "I'm sorry. I'm not great at handling so much coming at me so fast."

"Maude? Relatives?"

"And you."

In a matter of weeks his entire life had changed. Not to most observers, but inside, in his heart and mind, everything had shifted. Between Maude and Olive, he hadn't had a chance.

He reached into his pocket and pulled out the small gray bag.

"Are those..."

"Yes. Maude's earrings. The ones she wants me to give to the woman I love." He leaned in and kissed her. Damn, he'd wanted to do this for days. Since their night together had ended, since he'd realized how important she was to him and backed away because backing away was easier than sticking around and getting the shaft.

*Take a chance. Put it all on the line.*

"These are for you," he said. "My grandmother wants me to give them to the woman I love, and that's you, Olive. It will always be you. Take them."

Her response was to wrap her arms around his neck and kiss him again. She laughed lightly against his lips, held on tight, and when she pulled away, he saw that her eyes glistened with tears.

"Are those tears of joy or..."

She took the earrings from his hand. "I love you, too."

This was all well and good, but there were still obstacles in their way. For the first time in his life, he was certain there were no obstacles they couldn't overcome.

"When do you go back to Birmingham?" he asked. "I can leave The Magnolia in good hands and be out of here in a couple of weeks."

"That won't be necessary," she said.

His heart dropped until she continued. "I'm not going back. Well, I'll have to make a trip to finish up some business and get my stuff, but I'm about to become a Seawolf Beach resident. By mid-year the Sugar Plum Dance Academy should be up and running."

*But she didn't dance.*

Before he could respond Ava, still in her fairy costume, ran into the room. "Stop yelling!" she said.

Olive responded gently. "We're not yelling."

"Not you," Ava said, lifting one arm to point to one side. "Her! She says her name is Granny Maude."

"I thought she never left the depot," Tuck whispered.

Olive nodded. "That's what Anna said."

"Granny Maude wants to say bye, and she wants you to dance."

"Now?" Olive asked.

Ava nodded vigorously.

Andy Williams was back on the record player. The crooner's version of "Have Yourself a Merry Little Christmas," drifted into the kitchen. Tuck took Olive in his arms, and they began to move. "Sorry. I know you don't dance."

She smiled at him. "I can dance now. I *want* to dance. With you."

He lifted Olive off her feet and swung her around. She laughed; he laughed.

Ava left the room, running as always. He couldn't see her, but somehow he knew Maude was gone, too. She was no longer trapped, no longer caught between worlds.

His grandmother was where she was meant to be, and so was he.

The dance continued. He leaned in to brush his lips against a tempting earlobe, to kiss the neck just below, as he whispered,

"Olive, love, I will never drop you."

# ABOUT LINDA

Linda Winstead Jones is the New York Times and USA Today bestselling author of more than eighty romance novels and novellas across several sub-genres. She's easily distracted by new characters and ideas and writes the stories that speak to her in the moment. Paranormal. Romantic Suspense. Twisted Fairy Tales. Cowboys. Her books are for readers who want to escape from reality for a while, who don't mind the occasional trip into another world for a laugh, a chill, the occasional heartwarming tear. Where will we go next?

Sign up for Linda's newsletter on her website,
www.lindawinsteadjones.com

## ALSO BY LINDA WINSTEAD JONES

*Seawolf Beach*

Ghost Town Boogie

Sugar Plum Serenade

*Mystic Springs*

Bigfoot and the Librarian

Santa and the Snow Witch, a novella

Beauty and the Beastmaster

Ivy's Fall

Mystic Matchmaker, a short story

Last Call at the Doghouse

*For more, visit Linda's website at www.lindawinsteadjones.com.*